CONTEMPORARY AMERICAN FICTION

THE DEAD FATHER

Donald Barthelme has published twelve books, including two novels and a prize-winning children's book. He is a regular contributor to *The New Yorker* and divides his time between New York and Houston, where he teaches creative writing at the University of Houston. His collection of short stories *Overnight to Many Distant Cities* is available from Penguin.

The Dead Father

DONALD BARTHELME

PENGUIN BOOKS

PENGUIN BOOKS

Viking Penguin Inc., 40 West 23rd Street,
New York, New York 10010, U.S.A.
Penguin Books Ltd, Harmondsworth,
Middlesex, England
Penguin Books Australia Ltd, Ringwood,
Victoria, Australia
Penguin Books Canada Limited, 2801 John Street,
Markham, Ontario, Canada L3R 1B4
Penguin Books (N.Z.) Ltd, 182–190 Wairau Road,
Auckland 10, New Zealand

First published in the United States of America by
Farrar, Straus, and Giroux 1975
Published in Penguin Books 1986

A part of this novel originally appeared
in somewhat different form in *The New Yorker*.

LIBRARY OF CONGRESS CATALOGING IN PUBLICATION DATA
Barthelme, Donald.
The dead father.
I. Title.
PS3552.A76D4   1986   813'.54   85-28351
ISBN 0 14 00.8667 6

Printed in the United States of America by
R. R. Donnelley & Sons Company, Harrisonburg, Virginia
Set in Primer

For Marion

THE DEAD FATHER

The Dead Father's head. The main thing is, his eyes are open. Staring up into the sky. The eyes a two-valued blue, the blues of the Gitanes cigarette pack. The head never moves. Decades of staring. The brow is noble, good Christ, what else? Broad and noble. And serene, of course, he's dead, what else if not serene? From the tip of his finely shaped delicately nostriled nose to the ground, fall of five and one half meters, figure obtained by triangulation. The hair is gray but a young gray. Full, almost to the shoulder, it is possible to admire the hair for a long time, many do, on a Sunday or other holiday or in those sandwich hours neatly placed between fattish slices of work. Jawline compares favorably to a rock formation. Imposing, rugged, all that. The great jaw contains thirty-two teeth, twenty-eight of the whiteness of standard bathroom fixtures and four stained, the latter a consequence of addiction to tobacco, according to legend, this beige quartet to be found in the center of the lower jaw. He is not perfect, thank God for that. The full red lips drawn back in a slight rictus, slight but not unpleasant rictus, disclosing a bit of mackerel salad lodged between two of the stained four. We think it's mackerel salad. It appears to be mackerel salad. In the sagas, it is mackerel salad.

Dead, but still with us, still with us, but dead.

No one can remember when he was not here in our city

3

positioned like a sleeper in troubled sleep, the whole great expanse of him running from the Avenue Pommard to the Boulevard Grist. Overall length, 3,200 cubits. Half buried in the ground, half not. At work ceaselessly night and day through all the hours for the good of all. He controls the hussars. Controls the rise, fall, and flutter of the market. Controls what Thomas is thinking, what Thomas has always thought, what Thomas will ever think, with exceptions. The left leg, entirely mechanical, said to be the administrative center of his operations, working ceaselessly night and day through all the hours for the good of all. In the left leg, in sudden tucks or niches, we find things we need. Facilities for confession, small booths with sliding doors, people are noticeably freer in confessing to the Dead Father than to any priest, of course! he's dead. The confessions are taped, scrambled, recomposed, dramatized, and then appear in the city's theaters, a new feature-length film every Friday. One can recognize moments of one's own, sometimes.

The right foot rests at the Avenue Pommard and is naked except for titanium steel band around ankle, this linked by titanium steel chains to dead men (**dead man** n. 1. a log, concrete block, etc., buried in the ground as an anchor) to the number of eight sunk in the green of the Gardens. There is nothing unusual about the foot except that it is seven meters high. The right knee is not very interesting and no one has ever tried to dynamite it, tribute to the good sense of the citizens. From the knee to the hip joint (Belfast Avenue) everything is most ordinary. We encounter for example the rectus femoris, the saphenous nerve, the iliotibial tract, the femoral artery, the vastus medialis, the vastus lateralis, the vastus intermedius, the gracilis, the adductor magnus, the adductor longus, the intermediate femoral cutaneous nerve and other simple premechanical devices of this nature. All working night and day for the good of all. Tiny arrows are found in the right leg, sometimes. Tiny arrows are *never found in the left (artificial) leg at any time, tribute to the good sense of the citizens. We want the Dead Father to be dead. We sit with tears in our eyes wanting the Dead Father to be dead—meanwhile doing amazing things with our hands.*

1

Eleven o'clock in the morning. The sun doing its work in the sky.

The men are tiring, said Julie. Perhaps you should give them a break.

Thomas made the "break" signal waving his arm in a downward motion.

The men fell out by the roadside. The cable relaxed in the road.

This grand expedition, the Dead Father said, this waltz across an unknown parquet, this little band of brothers . . .

You are not a brother, Julie reminded him. Do not get waltzed away.

That they should so love me, the Dead Father said, as to haul and haul and haul and haul, through the long days and nights and less than optimal weather conditions . . .

Julie looked away.

My children, the Dead Father said. Mine. Mine. Mine.

Thomas lay down with his head in Julie's lap.

Many sad things have befallen me, he said, and many sad things are yet to befall me, but the saddest thing of all is that fellow Edmund. The fat one.

6

The drunk, Julie said.

Yes.

How did you come by him?

I was standing in the square, on a beer keg as I re-member, signing people up, and heard this swallowing noise under my feet. Edmund. Swallowing the tap.

You knew, then. Before you signed him up.

He begged. He was abject.

A son of mine, nevertheless, said the Dead Father.

It would be the making of him, he said. Our march. I did not agree. But it is hard to deny someone the thing he thinks will be the making of him. I signed him up.

He has handsome hair, Julie said. That I've noticed.

He was happy to throw away the cap-and-bells, said Thomas. As we all were, he added, looking pointedly at the Dead Father.

Thomas pulled an orange fool's cap tipped with silver bells from his knapsack.

To think that I have worn this abomination, or its mate, since I was sixteen.

Sixteen to sixty-five, so says the law, said the Dead Father.

This does not make you loved.

Loved! Not a matter of love. A matter of Organization.

All the little heads so gay, said Julie. Makes one look a perfect fool, the cap. Brown-and-beige, maroon-and-gray, red-and-green, all bells chilattering. What a picture. I thought, What perfect fools.

As was intended, said the Dead Father.

And had I been caught out-of-doors without it, my ears cut off, said Thomas. What a notion. What an imagination.

A certain artistry, said the Dead Father. In my ukases.

Let us lunch, said Julie. Although it's early.

The roadside. The tablecloth. Ringle of dinnerbell. Toasted prawns. They disposed themselves around the cloth in this fashion:

7

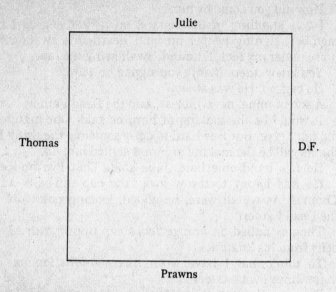

Julie

Thomas   D.F.

Prawns

Quite good.
Not so bad.
Is there mustard?
In the pot.
Something in it.
What?
Look there.
Pick it out with your finger.
Nasty little bugger.
Pass the prawns.
And for dessert?
Fig Newtons.

They sat contentedly around the cloth, munching. Ahead of them, the lunch fires of the men. The cable slack in the roadway.

Soon we will be there, said the Dead Father.

Fourteen days or fifteen days, I reckon, Thomas said. If we are headed right.

Is there any doubt?

There is always doubt.

When we are there, and when I wrap myself in its warm yellowness, then I will be young again, said the Dead Father. I shall once more be wiry.

Wiry! Julie exclaimed. She stuffed a part of the tablecloth into her mouth.

My dear, Thomas said. He extended a hand which of itself and without guidance grasped one of her handsome breasts.

Not in front of him.

Thomas removed the hand.

Can you tell us, he asked, what that hussar had done? The one we saw hanged by the neck from the tree back down the road a bit.

Disobeyed a ukase, said the Dead Father. I forget which ukase.

Oh, said Thomas.

Nobody disobeys a ukase of mine, said the Dead Father. He chuckled.

Smug, isn't he, said Julie.

A bit smug, said Thomas.

A bit, the Dead Father said.

They gazed at each other fondly. Three fond gazes roving like searchlights across the prawns.

They packed up. Thomas gave the signal. The cable jerked. The sun still. Trees. Vegetation. Wild gooseberries. Weather.

I'll let you have a wipe of it sometimes, the Dead Father said. Both of you.

Thanks, Julie said.

When I embrace or am embraced by its damned fine luster, the Dead Father said, all this will seem worthwhile.

He paused.

Even the cable.

Another pause.

Even those galoots you hired to haul on the cable.

Volunteers, every one, Thomas said. Delighted to be in your service. To be wearing your livery.

No matter. When I clutch its fine golden strands to my ancient bosom—

His hopes are got up, I'm afraid, Julie said.

Thomas flang his sword into a bush.

It's not fair! he exclaimed.

What's not fair?

Why do I feel so bad? he asked, looking round him in every direction, as if for an answer.

Are you ill?

I could use a suck of the breast, Thomas said.

Not in front of him.

They retired from the Dead Father's view, behind a proliferation of Queen Anne's lace. Julie seated herself on the ground and opened her blouse. Two bold breasts presented themselves, the left a little smaller than the right but just as handsome in its own way.

Ah! said Thomas, after a time. Nothing like a suck of the breast. Is there more?

While I live, beloved.

Thomas indulged himself further.

Julie buttoned her blouse. They emerged hand-in-hand from the Queen Anne's lace, Thomas swabbing his chops with the hand that was not hand-in-hand.

A bit left out, said the Dead Father. A bit. That is what I feel, at this moment.

Suffer, said Thomas, reclaiming his sword from the bush.

Excluded, said the Dead Father.

It is because you are an old fart, Julie explained. Old farts don't get much.

The Dead Father leaped to his feet and stormed off

10

down the road, upon receiving this information. His golden robes flaring all about him. The cable trailing.

He has slipped his cable, said Thomas.

They stormed off after him. When they caught up, they found a terrible scene.

The Dead Father was slaying, in a grove of music and musicians. First he slew a harpist and then a performer upon the serpent and also a banger upon the rattle and also a blower of the Persian trumpet and one upon the Indian trumpet and one upon the Hebrew trumpet and one upon the Roman trumpet and one upon the Chinese trumpet of copper-covered wood. Also a blower upon the marrow trumpet and one upon the slide trumpet and one who wearing upon his head the skin of a cat performed upon the menacing murmurous cornu and three blowers on the hunting horn and several blowers of the conch shell and a player of the double aulos and flautists of all descriptions and a Panpiper and a fagotto player and two virtuosos of the quail whistle and a zampogna player whose fingering of the chanters was sweet to the ear and by-the-bye and during a rest period he slew four buzzers and a shawmist and one blower upon the water jar and a clavicytheriumist who was before he slew her a woman, and a stroker of the theorbo and countless nervous-fingered drummers as well as an archlutist, and then whanging his sword this way and that the Dead Father slew a cittern plucker and five lyresmiters and various mandolinists, and slew too a violist and a player of the kit and a picker of the psaltery and a beater of the dulcimer and a hurdy-gurdier and a player of the spike fiddle and sundry kettledrummers and a triangulist and two-score finger cymbal clinkers and a xylophone artist and two gongers and a player of the small semantron who fell with his iron hammer still in his hand and a trictrac specialist and a marimbist and a maracist and a falcon drummer and a sheng blower and a sansa pusher and a manipulator of the gilded ball.

11

The Dead Father resting with his two hands on the hilt of his sword, which was planted in the red and steaming earth.

My anger, he said proudly.

Then the Dead Father sheathing his sword pulled from his trousers his ancient prick and pissed upon the dead artists, severally and together, to the best of his ability—four minutes, or one pint.

Impressive, said Julie, had they not been pure cardboard.

My dear, said Thomas, you deal too harshly with him.

I have the greatest possible respect for him and for what he represents, said Julie, let us proceed.

They proceeded.

2

The countryside. Flowers. Creeping snowberry. The road with dust. The sweat popping from little sweat glands. The line of the cable.

Beautiful country around here, said Julie.

Gorgeous, said Thomas.

Great to be alive, said the Dead Father. To breathe in and out. To feel one's muscles bite and snap.

How is your leg? Thomas asked. The mechanical one.

It is incomparable, said the Dead Father. Magnificent, that would be a word for it. I would I had two as good as the left. Old Plugalong.

How did you come by it? asked Thomas. Accident or design?

The latter, said the Dead Father. In my vastness, there was room for, necessity of, every kind of experience. I therefore decided that mechanical experience was a part of experience there was room for, in my vastness. I wanted to know what machines know.

What do machines know?

Machines are sober, uncomplaining, endlessly efficient, and work ceaselessly through all the hours for the good of all, said the Dead Father. They dream, when they dream, of stopping. Of last things. They—

What's that? Thomas interrupted. He was pointing to the side of the road.

13

Two children. One male. One female. Not too big. Not too small. Holding hands.

Children in love, said Julie.

In love? How do you know?

I have an eye for love, she said, and there it is. A clear instance.

Children, said the Dead Father. Whippersnappers.

What is that? the children asked, pointing to the Dead Father.

That is a Dead Father, Thomas told them.

The children hugged each other tightly.

He doesn't look dead to us, said the girl.

He is walking, said the boy. Or standing up, anyhow.

He is dead only in a sense, Thomas said.

The children kissed each other, on the lips.

They don't seem very impressed, said the Dead Father. Where is the awe?

They are lost in each other, said Julie. Soaks up all available awe.

Don't seem old enough, Thomas said. How old are you? he asked.

We are twenty, said the girl. I am ten and he is ten. Old enough. We are going to live together all our lives and love each other all our lives until we die. We know it. But don't tell anyone because we'll be beaten, if the knowledge becomes general.

Aren't they supposed to be throwing rocks at each other at this age? Thomas asked.

Always magnificent exceptions, Julie said.

We have cut our fingers with an X-Acto knife and mingled our bloods, the boy said.

Two tiny forefingers with short crusty cuts exhibited.

Did you sterilize the knife? I hope? Julie asked.

We dangled it in the vodka bottle, said the girl, I judged that sufficient.

That would do it, Thomas said.

14

We will never be parted. I am Hilda and he is Lars. When he is eighteen he is going to refuse to do his military service and I am going to do something so I can be put in the same jail with him, I haven't thought it up yet.

Admirable, Julie said.

We are together, said Hilda, and will always be. You are too old to know how it is.

I am?

You must be about twenty-six.

Exactly.

And he is even older, she said, indicating Thomas.

Considerably, Thomas admitted.

And *he,* she pointed to the Dead Father, must be, I can't imagine. Maybe a hundred.

Wrong, the Dead Father said gaily. Wrong, but close. Even older than that, but also younger. Having it both ways is a thing I like.

All this age fills up your heads, Hilda said. So you cannot remember what it was like, being a child. Probably you don't even remember the fear. So much of the *it.* So little of you. The lunge under the blanket.

There is still more of the it than there is of me, said Thomas. But one gets along reasonably well.

Reasonably, said the girl, what a word.

The children began caressing each other, with hands and cheeks and hair.

Do we have to witness this? asked the Dead Father. This gross physicality?

You are in a new world, Thomas said. Nine-year-olds are arrested for rape. This is not that. Be grateful.

Dyscrasia, the Dead Father said, that is what I think of it. Pathological. I shall issue a ukase against it.

Are you in school? Julie asked the children.

Of course we are in school, Hilda said. Why does everyone always ask a child if he or she is in school? We are all in school. There is no way to excape.

15

Do you want to excape?

Didn't you?

What do you study in school?

We are invigorated with the sweet sensuality of language. We learn to make sentences. Come to me. May I come to your house? Christmas comes but once a year. I'll come to your question. The light comes and goes. Success comes to those who strive. Tuesday comes after Monday. Her aria comes in the third act. Toothpaste comes in a tube. Peaches come from trees and good results do not come from careless work. This comes of thoughtlessness. The baby came at dawn. She comes from Warsaw. He comes from a good family. It will come easy with a little practice. I'll come to thee by moonlight, though—

I think this child is a bit of a smart-ass, said the Dead Father. I shall cause her to be sent to a Special School and her rusty-mouthed companion there also.

If you do that we shall leap into the reservoir, Lars said, together. And drown. I am going to tell you something utterly astounding, surprising, marvelous, miraculous, triumphant, astonishing, unheard of, singular, extraordinary, incredible, unforeseen, vast, tiny, rare, common, glaring, secret until today, brilliant and enviable; in short something unexampled in previous ages except for one single instance which is not really comparable; something we find impossible to believe in Paris (so how could anyone in Lyons believe it?), something which makes everyone exclaim aloud in amazement, something which causes the greatest joy to those who know of it, something, in short, which will make you doubt the evidence of your senses: We don't care what you think.

I am offended, said the Dead Father.

I was quoting Mme de Sévigné, said the boy, except for the last part, which was mine.

16

These children are tuned a little fine, the Dead Father said, a Special School is the answer.

Is that the kind that looks like a zoo?

There are cages, yes. But we have been experimenting with moats.

No way, the children said.

The children standing and washing each other with their active hands.

I cannot bear to look longer, said Julie, let us proceed.

These are odd children, Thomas said, but all children are odd children, rightly regarded.

Shout of Thomas to the men: Resume, resume!

Tightening of the cable.

Small gifts to the children: a power mower, a Blendor.

They will need them in their long lives together, Thomas explained.

Goodbye! Goodbye! the children shouted. Don't tell, please don't tell, never tell, never tell, please!

We won't we won't we won't! they shouted back. The Dead Father did not shout.

Children, he said. Without children I would not be the Father. No Fatherhood without childhood. I never wanted it, it was thrust upon me. Tribute of a sort but I could have done without, fathering then raising each one of the thousands and thousands and tens of thousands, the inflation of the little bundle to big bundle, period of years, and then making sure the big bundles if male wore their cap-and-bells, and if not observed the principle of jus primae noctis, the embarrassment of sending away those I didn't want, the pain of sending away those I did want, out into the lifestream of the city, nevermore to warm my cold couch, and the management of the hussars, maintenance of public order, keeping the zip codes straight, keeping the fug out of the gutters, would have preferred remaining in my study comparing editions of Klinger, the first state, the second state, the third state, and so on, was

17

there parting along the fold? and so on, water stain and so on, but this was not possible, all went forth and multiplied, and multiplied, and multiplied, and I had to Father, it was the natural order, thousands, tens of thousands, but I wanted to wonder if if if I put a wood pulp mat next to a 100 percent rag print would there be foxing and whether the rumblings of the underground would shake the chalk dust from my pastels or not. I never wanted it, it was thrust upon me. I wanted to worry about the action of the sun fading what I valued most, strong browns turning to pale browns if not vacant yellows, how to protect against, that sort of thing, but no, I had to devour them, hundreds, thousands, feefifofum, sometimes their shoes too, get a good mouthful of childleg and you find, between your teeth, the poisoned sneaker. Hair as well, millions of pounds of hair scarifying the gut over the years, why couldn't they have just been thrown down wells, exposed on hillsides, accidentally electrocuted by model railroads? And the worst was their blue jeans, my meals course after course of improperly laundered blue jeans, T-shirts, saris, Thom McAns. I suppose I could have hired someone to peel them for me first.

Believe me, the Dead Father said, I never wanted it, I wanted only the comfort of my armchair, the feel of a fine Fabriano paper, the cool anxiety about whether I had been cogged if if if with a restrike or not, whether some cunning fellow had steelfaced an old copperplate and run off the odd thousand extra impressions, whether a thing was by Master HL or Master HB or if if if if—

He does go on, said Julie.

And on and on and on, said Thomas. However he is bearing up remarkably well.

He *is* bearing up remarkably well.

I am bearing up remarkably well, said the Dead Father, because I have hope.

Tell me, said Julie, did you ever want to paint or draw or etch? Yourself?

18

It was not necessary, said the Dead Father, because I am the Father. All lines my lines. All figure and all ground mine, out of my head. All colors mine. You take my meaning.

We had no choice, said Julie.

3

A halt. The men lay down the cable. The men regard
Julie from a distance. The men standing about. Pemmican measured out in great dark whacks from the pem-
mican-whacking knife. Edmund lifts flask to lips. Thomas
removes flask. Protest by Edmund. Reproof from Thomas.
Julie gives Edmund a chaw of bhang. Gratitude of Edmund. Julie wipes Edmund's forehead with white handkerchief. The cable relaxed in the road. The blue of the
sky. Trees leant against. Bird stutter and the whisper of
grasses. The Dead Father playing his guitar. Thomas performing leadership functions. Construction of the plan.
Maps pored over and the sacred beans bounced in the
pot. The yarrow sticks cast. The dice cup given a shake.
Shoulder blade of a sheep roasted and the cracks in the
bone read. Peas agitated in a sieve. The hatchet struck
into a great stake and its quivers recorded. First-sprouting
onion caught and its peels palpated. Portents totted up
and divided by seven. Thomas falls to the ground in a
swoon.

Picking up of Thomas. The Dead Father pauses in mid-
strum. Application of wet cloths to Thomas's forebrain.
He revives. Anxiety of the onlookers. What has been
foretold? Whacks of pemmican poised over open mouths
in anticipation of revelation. Thomas remains silent.

Anger of the men. Thomas stares at shoes. Anger of the men. Edmund lifts flask to lips. Emma appears. Thomas is startled. Who is Emma? Emma sits down on a box. Julie regards Emma. Her stare met. Two stares contending. Emma fingering her brooch. Julie standing with hands pressed into thighs, atop skirt. Thomas fiddling with sword hilt. Silence of the troops. Golden hair of Emma. Pouty bosom of Emma. Merry eye of Emma. General consternation. The Dead Father lists his degrees. B.S.A., Bachelor of Science in Agriculture, to B.S.S.S., Bachelor of Science in Secretarial Studies. Evil look from Thomas to the Dead Father. Ferns cut and on a bed of ferns fresh trout newly wrest from the trout stream presented to Emma by kneeling-on-one-knee troopers. Emma pleased. Little hairs of pleasure rise on back of Emma's neck. Emma suggests cooking of trout (immediate) and produces from reticule a can of slivered almonds. The men build a fire, all pemmican forgot. More trout persuaded from trout stream, they are very eager. The sky grays as sun zips behind large cloud. Waning or demise of sun. The projector is set up for projection of the pornographic film. Thomas decides that the Dead Father is not allowed to view film, because of his age. Outrage of the Dead Father. Death of the guitar, whanged against a tree, in outrage. Guitar carcass added to the fire. Thomas adamant. The Dead Father raging. Emma regnant. Julie staring. Trout browning. Thomas walks to the edge. Regards the edge. Aspect of one about to hurtle over the. Thomas retreats from the edge. Slivered almonds distributed over various trouts browning in various skillets. Projector casts image upon screen (collapsible/portable). The Dead Father led away and chained to an engine block abandoned in a farther field. Revilings by the Dead Father. Damn your eyes, etc. Ignoring by Thomas. The film. Scenes of partying, men and women, the fourth guest, a woman, gets up and sits in the lap of

21

the second guest, a woman, they begin fondling each other's breasts. The ninth guest, a man, approaches the sixth guest (the one kneeling with her head between the legs of the fifth guest) and begins taking off her jeans. The ninth guest unbuckles the sixth guest's belt, unzips the jeans, and works them down over her hips. The ninth guest carefully pulls down the sixth guest's panties, which are orange, and sticks his erect thumb between her legs. Some members of the group watching screen, some watching Emma, some watching Emma/screen/Emma/screen, some watching Emma/screen/Julie/screen/Thomas.

Beam of Emma touching every face and who knows? heart. Tilt of Emma-bust toward fire where it blushes in the firelight. Frown from Julie who is removing small bones from trout. Seating arrangements to be announced. Beam of Emma creating confusions, some return beam, some do not, some are sunk in film, some asprawl in each other's arms for mutual solace and comfort, some creeping toward Emma's box on hands and knees, when—

Emma rises, stretches out hands. Receives her trout brown and toasty with its little flittered almonds in a tasty sauce, butter, herbs. Emma bites trout. Bite-hole in trout, U-shaped. Applause of the men. Banging together of hands. Thomas orders the film ceased. The film, he says, does not represent accurately the parameters of human love. Something missing, he says. Anger of the men. Thomas discourses for fifteen minutes upon the subject, his own (personal) love of pornography. Nevertheless this film, this film, he says, is turned off. The sixth guest begins to move slowly up and down upon the thumb of the ninth guest and the picture is white light. Anger of the men. Anger of the women. Whistles and stomps. Ranting of the Dead Father, from a farther field. Thomas walks again toward the edge.

Absence of film. Restlessness of the men. The bolder

22

come closer. Emma's box upon which Emma's funda-
ment rests closely regarded. Attempt by the boldest to in-
sinuate head under Emma's skirts, there to witness who
knows what. These unsuccessful, Emma's dainty foot
kicks. That will teach them. Chomping on trout continues
the while, some sillybaby also chomped, with a dill sauce.
That will teach them. Grumbling intermixed with shrieks.
Emma rises, stretches. Then the duel, Alexander vs. Sam.
Each pinks the other in the shoulder. Thomas bandaid-
ing. Julie moves to Emma. Conversation.

Whose little girl are you?
I get by, I get by.
Time to go.
Hoping this will reach you at a favorable moment.
Bad things can happen to people.
Is that a threat?
Dragged him all this distance without any rootytoot-
toot.
Is that a threat?
Take it any way you like it.
Other fish to fry.
We guarantee every effort will be made.
Who's the boss?
One in the orange tights.
He's not bad-looking.
That's one opinion.
Inclined to tarry for a bit.
Pop one of these if you'd like a little lift.
Thank you.
Two is one too many.
That's your opinion.
Since you have not as yet responded to my suggestion.
Where are you taking him?
We guarantee every effort will be made.
More than I can bear.
No it's not.

Frightful violation of the ordinaries.
No it's not.
He's not bad-looking.
Haven't made up my mind.
You must have studied English.
Take my word for it.
How did that make you feel?
Wasn't the worst.
I queened it for a while in Yorkshire.
Did you know Lord Raglan?
I knew Lord Raglan.
He's not bad-looking.
Handsome, clever, rich.
Yorkshire has no queen of its own I believe.
Correct.
Time to go.
Inclined to tarry for a bit. Thank you.
Two is one too many.
That's your opinion.
Nevertheless. Nevertheless.
Various circumstances requiring my attention.
I can make it hot for you.
So full and orange.
You don't know what you're getting into.
Hoping this will reach you at a favorable moment.
Wake up one dark night with a thumb in your eye.
Women together changing that which can and ought
to be changed.
Dangled his twiddle-diddles in my face.
More than I can bear.
No it's not.
Will it hurt?
I don't know, I don't know, I don't know.
He's not bad-looking.
Haven't made up my mind.
Groups surrounding us needing direction.

Maybe.

What's he like?

That's my business.

Have you tried any of the others?

That's my business.

Want to take a look around. See the sights.

I can make it hot for you.

Is that a threat?

Construed any way you wish.

I asked him about organization.

What did he tell you?

Destroy it in order to let the water flow freely.

That's referred pain I know about that.

But a maiden drowned.

Did they recover a body?

Three. Two were the bodies of sheep.

Oh yes I read about it. In the *Svenska Dagbladet*.

And he felt guilty.

I never asked him.

It's all been carefully considered.

He's a motherfucker I tell you true.

Nevertheless.

Doing what we must at great personal and emotional cost.

Any of the others any good?

Haven't tried them.

Thought I heard a dog barking.

It's possible. The simplest basic units develop into the richest natural patterns.

Are you into spanking?

No I'm not.

Pity. We could have got something going.

I'm not into that.

Where can a body get a hit around here?

Pop one of these if you'd like a little lift.

Thank you. Palm Sunday.

Hope you know what you're doing. Cordially.
Not too bothered. Thank you.
Time to go, time to go.
Walking by the sea, listening to the waves.
Think I'm getting nosebleed.
Have my handkerchief.
I've one of my own thank you.
I could have put it in a brick, he said.
A filthy-mouthed man.
He's not bad-looking.
Have you tried any of the others?
I am only recently arrived and would like to wash and
rest a bit.
Every effort will be made. I can make it hot for you.
Will it hurt?
My discretion. My yea or nay.
Thought I heard a dog barking.
A spiritual aridity quite hard to reconcile with his sur-
face gaiety.
Left Barcelona in disgrace.
I was suspicious of him from the first.
Certain provocations the government couldn't handle.
Too early to tell. That's a very handsome pin.
My mother's. Willed to me at her death.
Goodbye goodbye goodbye.
Think I'll stick around for a while.
That's interesting.
Take the lay of the land.
That's interesting.
Have you told him?
To my shame I have not.
And if it is at all possible for you to see me.
Fond urgings and soft petitions.
It's all been carefully considered.
What?
Thought I heard a dog barking.
Did you know Lord Raglan?

26

We nodded when our carriages passed.
Out of here, out of here.
Not today, not today.
Pop one of these it will give you a little lift.
Will it hurt?

4

The line of march. Line of the cable. Viewed from above,
this picture:

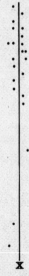

x

They came then to a man tending bar in an open field.
Yes, Thomas said.
Relaxation of the cable.
Drinks for everyone.

Ah! said Thomas.

Not too bad, said the Dead Father.

Yum, said Emma.

Another, Thomas said.

That was vodka, right? the bartender asked.

On the rocks and could I have three olives?

Three olives, said the bartender.

Having made the drinks he folded his arms and leaned against a tree.

Did you see the horses? asked the Dead Father.

Clump of eight, Julie said. I counted.

Black plumes, Thomas said. Black bridles, black trappings.

Black horses, said the Dead Father.

Standing in a rank, very well trained, not a whicker.

Perhaps they weren't real? asked the Dead Father.

They were real, said Thomas.

Julie ordered another drink.

You've had enough, said the bartender, no more.

He's right, said Thomas, you've had enough.

I'll decide when I've had enough, Julie said. I want another.

He could lose his license if you fell down or committed an outrage, Thomas said.

That's true, said the bartender, I could lose my license.

Here? asked Julie, indicating the emptiness. Who is to be outraged?

One never knows, said the Dead Father. Thirsty pilgrims, natives of the district, commercial travelers.

Make it a double, said Julie.

We do not serve unaccompanied women, said the bartender.

I am accompanied am I not?

Do you mean the one in the orange tights or the one in the golden robes?

Both.

29

I saw him with his thumb under there, said the bartender, had his thumb on it I'll bet. Shocking rude I'd call it, in a public place.

Shocking, said the Dead Father happily. Never in all my years—

You're a family man, now, the bartender said to the Dead Father. That's perfectly plain.

Very much so.

You've children, said the bartender, responsibilities.

Beyond counting.

Thought so, said the bartender, I can talk to you. We understand each other.

Yes, fire away.

We can parley, said the bartender, make powwow.

Thomas was looking at the yellow sky.

Till the cows come home, said the Dead Father, so much are we on each other's wavelengths.

When he's got his thumb in there, asked the bartender, what do you feel?

Left out, said the Dead Father.

Button button who's got the button? chanted Julie. *I've* got the button.

Can I see it? asked the bartender.

Can I have another drink?

A double Scotch appeared on the bar.

Julie knocked back the Scotch. Then she removed her shirt. There was nothing under the shirt.

That's not what I meant, said the bartender, but God Almighty.

A crowd had gathered, both men and women. They were laughing.

Thomas smoothed Julie's stomach with his hand.

Don't touch! she said, you'll make the others angry.

The crowd stopped laughing, both men and women, moved nearer, was looking at Thomas with angry looks.

Who do you think you are? a man shouted angrily.

I am this lady's lover, Thomas shouted back.

30

Leave our stomach alone! the man shouted.

Your stomach? Thomas asked pointedly.

They crowded closer.

Hands were stretched out toward the stomach.

Mostly we don't get this kind of group, the bartender said.

Thomas began to write something with lipstick on the stomach. The white, interestingly folded, stomach.

Oh, you rascal! cried the crowd. Oh, you rogue!

Julie rotated the stomach at the crowd. Sunlight bouncing off the tips of her breasts (purple).

Emma sulking at the bar. Drinking a Campari-and-soda.

Thomas held out the shirt to Julie.

Our stomach! they said. He's taking it away!

The stomach heaved like a trampoline in the direction of its admirers.

Julie put on the shirt tucking the loose ends of it into her long dark-green skirt to the ground.

She looked at Thomas.

Have I lost my beauty altogether?

Not yet, he said.

Quite wonderful, said the Dead Father. I was offended, of course.

Suffer, Julie said.

The pink of you against the green of the fields, said Thomas. Several of my favorite colors.

They told me you were color-blind, when you were a boy, said the Dead Father. I never believed you were color-blind. A son of mine.

I thought I was color-blind, Thomas said, because they told me I was color-blind. To green, they said.

I never thought you were color-blind. You saw what we had agreed to call green.

I saw what I thought and still think was green.

Never thought you were color-blind or dim either, said the Dead Father, despite what I was told by the specialists.

31

You had hope, Thomas said. Grateful for that.

My criticism was that you never understood the larger picture, said the Dead Father. Young men never understand the larger picture.

I don't suggest I understand it now. I do understand the frame. The limits.

Of course the frame is easier to understand.

Older people tend to overlook the frame, even when they are looking right at it, said Thomas. They don't like to think about it.

Alexander approached Thomas.

Look there, he said. He pointed.

A horseman on the hill.

I think he's following us, said Alexander.

You've seen him before?

Yesterday. Always keeps the same distance.

Not one of those we passed back up the road?

No. Those were black, this is a bay.

I wonder who he is, Thomas said. He looked at the Dead Father's watch, which he was wearing on his wrist.

Okay, he said, let's make tracks.

The cable taut. The straggle along the road. The horseman following.

5

Thomas helping haul on the cable. Julie carrying the knapsack. The Dead Father eating a bowl of chocolate pudding.

When I asked you to help me, he said, it wasn't because I needed help.

Of course not, said Thomas.

I'm doing this for you, essentially, the Dead Father said. For the general good, and thus, for you.

Thomas said nothing.

As so much else, said the Dead Father.

Thomas said nothing.

You never knew, said the Dead Father.

Thomas turned his head.

You told us, he said, repeatedly.

Oh well yes I may have mentioned the odd initiative now and again. But you never *knew*. In the fullest sense. Because you are not a father.

I am, Thomas said. You forget Elsie.

Doesn't count, said the Dead Father. A son can never, in the fullest sense, become a father. Some amount of amateur effort is possible. A son may after honest endeavor produce what some people might call, technically, children. But he remains a son. In the fullest sense.

A moment's quiet.

Have you heard from her? Elsie?

There was a postcard, Thomas said, three months ago. Picture of a puppy dog with large staring eyes. Love, she said.

Four months ago, Julie said.

Three and a half months ago. She said she was playing field hockey. She was a left inner, she said.

Hockey, said the Dead Father. Chasing that round hard thing down the field. Develops the thigh muscles. Beyond what is desirable, sometimes.

Thomas jerked upon the cable. The Dead Father fell down. Julie and Emma picked him up.

Great knotted bunches of thigh muscles like a plate of red empty lobster shells, the Dead Father said, I can picture it. Antiaesthetic. Sad to see in a twelve-year-old.

I wrote that she was not to pursue it to excess, Thomas said, over his shoulder.

Why do you abide with him? the Dead Father said to Julie. A boy. A neonate. A weakwick. Probably not even found the button yet.

He's found it, she said.

Is it a large one? the Dead Father asked.

Large enough.

A tender red?

Tender enough.

Can I see it?

Oh I am tired of you! Julie cried.

She raised her arms with fists at the end into the air.

I am not tired of you, said the Dead Father.

That your tuff luck, she said. Not my tuff luck. Yours. Tuff titty.

Titty, said the Dead Father. A short suck?

You are incredible.

Thomas walked back to the Dead Father and rapped him sharply in the forehead.

The Dead Father said: This is damned unpleasant!

Then: If only I were myself again!

We are making progress, Thomas said.

34

When I douse myself in its great yellow electricity, the Dead Father said, then I will be revivified.

Best not to anticipate too much, said Thomas, it jiggles the possibilities.

Possibilities! Surely the Fleece is not a mere possibility?

It is an *excellent* possibility, Julie said quickly. A *wonderful* possibility.

Have you noticed the weather? asked Thomas.

All turned to look for the weather.

Good weather, Julie said. *Great* weather.

A very pleasant day, Emma noted.

Pleasant day, said the Dead Father.

Extremely pleasant, Thomas said.

It was on a day much like this, said the Dead Father, that I fathered the Pool Table of Ballambangjang.

The what?

It is rather an interesting tale, said the Dead Father, which I shall now tell. I had been fetched by the look of a certain maiden, a raven-haired maiden—

He looked at Julie, whose hand strayed to her dark dark hair.

A raven-haired maiden of great beauty. Her name was Tulla. I sent her many presents. Little machines, mostly, a machine for stamping her name on strips of plastic, a machine for extracting staples from documents, a machine for shortening her fingernails, a machine for removing wrinkles from fabric with the aid of steam. Well, she accepted the presents, no difficulty there, but me she spurned. Now as you might imagine I am not fond of being spurned. I am not used to it. In my domains it does not happen but as ill luck would have it she lived just over the county line. Spurned is not a thing I like to be. In fact I have a positive disinclination for it. So I turned myself into a haircut—

A haircutter? asked Julie.

A haircut, said the Dead Father. I turned myself into a haircut and positioned myself upon the head of a member

35

of my retinue, quite a handsome young man, younger than I, younger than I and stupider, that goes without saying, still not without a certain rude charm, bald as a bladder of lard, though, and as a consequence somewhat diffident in the presence of ladies. Using the long flowing sideburns as one would use one's knees in guiding a horse—

The horseman is still following us, Thomas noted. I wonder why.

—I sent him cantering off in the direction of the delectable Tulla, the Dead Father went on. So superior was the haircut, that is to say, me, joined together with his bumbly youngness, for which I do not blame him, that she succumbed immediately. Picture it. The first night. The touch nonesuch. At the crux I turned myself back into myself (vanishing the varlet) and we two she and I looked at each other and were content. We spent many nights together all roaratorious and filled with furious joy. I fathered upon her in those nights the poker chip, the cash register, the juice extractor, the kazoo, the rubber pretzel, the cuckoo clock, the key chain, the dime bank, the pantograph, the bubble pipe, the punching bag both light and heavy, the inkblot, the nose drop, the midget Bible, the slot-machine slug, and many other useful and humane cultural artifacts, as well as some thousands of children of the ordinary sort. I fathered as well upon her various institutions useful and humane such as the credit union, the dog pound, and parapsychology. I fathered as well various realms and territories all superior in terrain, climatology, laws and customs to this one. I overdid it but I was madly, madly in love, that is all I can say in my own defense. It was a very creative period but my darling, having mothered all this abundance uncomplainingly and without reproach, at last died of it. In my arms of course. Her last words were "enough is enough, Pappy." I was inconsolable and, driven as if

36

by a demon, descended into the underworld seeking to re-claim her.

I found her there, said the Dead Father, after many adventures too boring to recount. I found her there but she refused to return with me because she had already tasted the food-of-hell and grown fond of it, it's addicting. She was watched over by eight thunders who hovered over her and brought her every eve ever more hellish delicacies, and watched over furthermore by the ugly-men-of-hell who attacked me with dreampuffs and lyreballs and sought to drive me off. But I removed my garments and threw them at the ugly-men-of-hell, garment by garment, and as each garment touched even ever-so-slightly an ugly-man-of-hell he shriveled into a gasp of steam. There was no way I could stay, there was nothing to stay for, she was theirs.

Then to purify myself, said the Dead Father, of the impurities which had seeped into me in the underworld I dived headfirst into the underground river Jelly, I washed my left eye therein and fathered the deity Poolus who governs the progress of the ricochet or what bounces off what and to what effect, and washed my right eye and fathered the deity Ripple who has the governing of the happening of side effects/unpredictable. Then I washed my nose and fathered the deity Gorno who keeps tombs warm inside and the deity Libet who does not know what to do and is thus an inspiration to us all. I was then beset by eight hundred myriads of sorrows and sorrowing away when a worm wriggled up to me as I sat hair-tearing and suggested a game of pool. A way, he said, to forget. We had, I said, no pool table. Well, he said, are you not the Dead Father? I then proceeded to father the Pool Table of Ballambangjang, fashioning the green cloth of it from the contents of an alfalfa field nearby and the legs of it from telephone poles nearby and the dark pockets of it from the mouths of the leftover ugly-men-of-hell whom I bade

37

stand with their mouths open at the appropriate points—

What was the worm's name? Thomas asked.

I forget, said the Dead Father. Then, just as we were chalking our cues, the worm and I, Evil himself appeared, he-of-the-greater-magic, terrible in aspect, I don't want to talk about it, let me say only that I realized instantly that I was on the wrong side of the Styx. However I was not lacking in wit, even in this extremity. Uncoiling my penis, then in the dejected state, I made a long cast across the river, sixty-five meters I would say, where it snagged most conveniently in the cleft of a rock on the farther shore. Thereupon I hauled myself hand-over-hand 'midst excruciating pain as you can imagine through the raging torrent to the other bank. And with a hurrah! over my shoulder, to show my enemies that I was yet alive and kicking, I was off like a flash into the trees.

Infuckingcredible, said Julie.

Unfuckingbelievable, said Emma.

Rudolf Rassendyll himself could not have managed the affair better, said Thomas.

Yes, the Dead Father said, and on that bank of the river there stands to this day a Savings & Loan Association. A thing I fathered.

Forfuckingmidable, said Julie. I suddenly feel all mops and brooms.

Refuckingdoubtable, said Emma. I suddenly feel a saint of the saucepan.

Six and three quarters percent compounded momentarily, said the Dead Father, I guarantee it.

A bumaree, said Julie, they have this way of making you feel tiny and small.

They are good at it, said Emma.

We are only tidderly-push to the likes of them.

See themselves as a rope to the eye of a needle, said Emma.

It's a grin in a glass case, said Julie.

That was when I was young and full of that zest which

38

has leaked out of me and which we are journeying to recover for me by means of the great revitalizing properties of that long fleecy golden thing of which the bards sing and the skalds sing and the Meistersingers sing, said the Dead Father.

It is obvious that but for a twist of fate we and not they would be calling the tune, said Julie.

It is obvious that but for a twist of fate the mode of the music would be different, said Emma. Much different.

6

Evening. The campfire. Cats crying in the distance. Julie washing her shirt. Emma ordering her reticule.

Tell me a story, said the Dead Father.

Certainly, said Thomas. One day in a wild place far from the city four men in dark suits with shirts and ties and attaché cases containing Uzi submachine guns seized me, saying that I was wrong and had always been wrong and would always be wrong and that they were not going to hurt me. Then they hurt me, first with can openers then with corkscrews. Then, splashing iodine on my several wounds, they sped with me on horseback through the gathering gloom—

Oh! said the Dead Father. A dramatic narrative.

Very much so, said Thomas. They sped with me on horseback through the gathering gloom up the side of a small mountain, down the other side of the same mountain, across a small river, to an even wilder place still farther from the city. There, they proceeded to lunch. We lunched together with not a word spoken. Then, after policing the area down to the last chicken bone, we mounted once again and fled in single file through the damp mists of the afternoon over hills and dales and through hiatuses of various kinds, events perhaps I can't remember, to a yet wilder place rank with the odor of fish and the odor of dead grasses still farther from the city.

40

Here we watered the horses, against their will, they did not like the water. I helped make a fire gathering dry branches that had fallen from the trees but when I had finished helping make the fire I was told that no fire was wanted. Nevertheless one of the men opened his attaché case, withdrew his submachine gun and unfolding the folding stock fired a short burst into the dry branches setting them aflame. The horses reared and cried out in fear and the horseholder cursed the machine gunner and cursed me who had helped build a fire where no fire was wanted. Then, mounting once again and leaving the fire to do what it would among the creaking brownstained trees, we galloped down the center of a long valley through fields of winter wheat, leaping stones and fences to a house. Reining in there, we sat on our horses before the door of the house, horse breath visible in the chill of the evening, there was a light within. They escorted me into the house and by the dim illumination of a single candle hurt me again, with dinner forks. I asked for how many days or weeks or months was I to be thus transported and hurt and they said, until I accommodated. I asked them what that meant, accommodated, but they were silent.

We left the house and mounted again. Then, after galloping for some hours through the black of the night we came to a car wash. The car wash was made of steel and concrete block, we clattered through the entrance and past a mechanism wherein giant sponges were buffing late-model cars blue and gray and silver and behind that mechanism to a large room or ring with sand on the floor. I was taken from my horse by two men who bound my hands behind my back and thrust into my mouth a piece of paper on which was written something I could not see but which I knew had to do with me, was about me. Then I was pushed into the ring where wandered a dozen others similarly bound gripping between their teeth similar pieces of paper with things written on them, we walked or lurched around the ring avoiding bumping into each other but narrowly, when I came close to someone he or she made aggressive snarling gestures, I understood that we were to make aggressive snarling gestures, I made aggressive snarling gestures whenever one of them came near me meanwhile trying to read what was written on that person's piece of paper gripped between his or her teeth. But to no avail, I could not read what was written on any piece of paper although I did get a notion of the handwriting which was the same on every piece of paper, a fine thin cursive. This dree to-ing and fro-ing persisted throughout the night and through the next day and I became preoccupied with the thought, where was lunch? Having had lunch on the first day I expected it on the second and third and fourth but this was optimism, there was no lunch, only snarling aggressive gestures and attempts unsuccessful invariably to read what was written on the pieces of paper gripped in the mouths of my prancing colleagues. Then all-of-a-heap I was out of the ring and standing before a door, the door opened and I saw there two men on either side of a hospital bed atop which was a wood coffin containing a corpse dead I assumed, the corpse's hands were erect in the air clutching and I noticed that the fingers on each hand were missing, the corpse clutched with no fingers, the door closed and there was a sound as of a lift, the door opened again and the two men were gone and the corpse was gone. I stepped through the door into the lift and the door closed behind me. I was taken to the top floor.

I was taken to the top floor, Thomas said, there I found behind a desk a man in a mask. The mask was as tall as the man and had been hewn from a tree, it was African in character and had been worked upon with chisels most skillfully or perhaps with hoe blades most skillfully, it resembled a human face in that five holes presented themselves, there were no ears. The man in the mask said that I was wrong and had always been wrong and would al-

42

ways be wrong and that he was not going to hurt me. Then he hurt me, with documents. Then he asked my companions if I was maturing. He's growing older, the taller of the two replied, and everyone present nodded, this was certainly true, the man in the mask expressed satisfaction. Then, wrapping me in a djellabah of thirty shades of brown they removed me to a Land-Rover which immediately rovered out onto a broad arid plain for a distance of several hundred miles, stopping at intervals to take on petrol and water in battered jerry cans wrung from unwilling unbuttoned overweight out-of-uniform supply sergeants at depots along the route. Where was lunch? I wondered remembering the first day, the chicken, the cucumbers, the potato salad. On the other side of the desert we came to a swamp, great sucky grasses tufted into a green scum, we abandoned the Land-Rover for a pirogue, and with one of my companions paddling in the bow and the other poling in the stern and me in the middle set off across the dank whining surface, giant cypresses gnarling and snarling all about us and two-inch-high tree monkeys hanging by one arm like evil fruits therefrom. During a pause in the poling and pad-dling with the nose of the pirogue snugged into a greasy hummock they filled their pipes with damp tobacco drawn from their attaché cases, the which I was not offered any of, and damaged me again, with harsh words. But they seemed to be tiring, I was hurt less than before, they told me I was wrong etc. but added that I was be-coming, by virtue of their kind attentions and the waning of the present century and the edifications of surface travel, less wrong than before. We were going to see the Great Father Serpent, they said, the Great Father Serpent would if I answered the riddle correctly grant me a boon but it was one boon to a customer and I would never answer the riddle correctly so my hopes, they said, should not be got up. I rehearsed in my mind all the riddles that I knew, trying to patch the right answer to the right riddle, while I was disordering my senses in this way we pushed off again into the filthy water, in the distance I could hear a roaring.

I'm fatigued, said the Dead Father.

Be of good courage, said Thomas, it ends soon.

The roaring they told me was the voice of the Great Father Serpent calling for the foreskins of the uninitiated but I was safe, my foreskin had been surrendered long ago, to a surgeon in a hospital. As we drew near through the tangling vines I perceived the outlines of a serpent of huge bigness which held in its mouth a sheet of tin on which something was written, the roars rattled the tin and I was unable to make out the message. My keepers hauled the pirogue onto the piece of ground on which the monster was resting and approached him most def-erentially as who would not, shouting into his ear that I had come to be tested by the riddle and win for myself a boon and that if he were willing they would proceed to robe him for the riddling. The Great Father Serpent nodded most graciously and opening his mouth let fall the sheet of tin which on its reverse had been polished to the brightness of a mirror. My escorts set up the mirror side in such a way that the creature could regard himself with love as the fussing-over proceeded, I wondering the while if it would be possible to creep underneath and read the writing there. First they wrapped the Great Father Serpent in fine smallclothes of softwhispering blush-colored changeable taffeta taken from a mahogany ward-robe of prodigious size located behind him, tussling for half an hour to cover his whole great length.

I like him, said the Dead Father, in that we are both long, very long.

Reserve judgment, said Thomas, we are not quite to the end.

Then they put on him, said Thomas, a kind of scarlet skirt stuffed with bombast and pleated and slashed so as to show a rich inner lining of a lighter scarlet, the two

44

scarlets together making a brave show at his slightest movement or undulation. The Great Father Serpent looked neither to the right nor to the left but stark ahead at his primrose image in the tin. Then they covered the upper or more headward length of him with a light jacket of white silk embroidered with a thread nutmeg in color and a thread goose-turd in color, these intertwined, and trimmed with fine whipped lace. Then they put on him a sort of doublet of silver brocade slashed with scarlet and slashed again with gold, sleeves for his no-arms hanging there picked out with seed pearls, the doublet having four and one half dozen buttons, the buttons being one dozen of ivory, one dozen of silk, one dozen of silk and hair, one dozen mixed gold and silver wire, and six diamonds set in gold. Next they put on him a great cloak made of un- shorn velvet pear-colored inside and outside embroidered at the top and down the back with bugles and pearls countless in number and holding two dozens of buttons, altogether they were near two hours a-buttoning, while they buttoned I inched closer to the underside of the tin which was taller than myself and leaning against a tree, I inched and inched, sometimes half-inched, so that to the eye my movements were imperceptible. Then they belted around his midpoint a girdle of russet gold with pearls and spangles supporting his hanger, to which was buckled the scabbard (buff-colored leather worked in silver wire gimp and colored silk) which held the shining, split tongue two meters long. As they placed upon the ob- long head the French hat with its massy goldsmith's work and long black feather, I slipped beneath the tin and out again, I could not believe what I saw written there. The Great Father Serpent nodded once at his own image, whisked the tongue from its scabbard, and pronounced himself ready to riddle.

Here is the riddle said the Great Father Serpent with a great flourishing of his two-tipped tongue, and it is a son- of-a-bitch I will tell you that, the most arcane item in the arcana, you will never guess it in a hundred thousand human years some of which I point out have already been used up by you in useless living and breathing but have a go, have a go, do: *What do you really feel?* Like murderinging, I answered, because that is what I had read on the underside of the tin, the wording *murderinging* inscribed in a fine thin cursive. Why bless my soul, said the Great Father Serpent, he's got it, and the two ruffians blinked at me in stunned wonder and I myself wondered, and marveled, but what I was wondering and marveling at was the closeness with which what I had answered accorded with my feelings, my lost feelings that I had never found before. I suppose, the Father Serpent said, that the boon you wish granted is the ability to carry out this foulness? Of course, I said, what else? Granted then, he said, but may I remind you that having the power is often enough. You don't have to actually do it. For the soul's ease. I thanked the Great Father Serpent; he bowed most cordially; my companions returned me to the city. I was abroad in the city with murderinging in mind—the dream of a stutterer.

That is a tall tale, said the Dead Father. I don't believe it ever happened.

No tale ever happened in the way we tell it, said Thomas, but the moral is always correct.

What is the moral?

Murderinging, Thomas said.

Murderinging is not correct, said the Dead Father. The sacred and noble Father should not be murdereded. Never. Absolutely not.

I mentioned no names, said Thomas.

He was staring at the Dead Father's belt buckle.

Very handsome buckle you have there, he said, I never noticed before.

The belt buckle was silver. Six inches square. A ruby or two.

The Dead Father regarded his belt buckle.

46

Gift of the citizens, many Father's Days ago. One of several hundred sumptuous offerings, on that Father's Day.

May I try it on? Thomas asked.

You want to try on my belt?

Yes I'd like to try it on if you don't mind.

You may certainly try it on if you wish.

The Dead Father unbuckled the belt and handed it to Thomas.

Thomas buckled on the Dead Father's belt.

I like it, he said. Yes, it looks well on me. The buckle. You may have the belt back, if you like.

My belt buckle! said the Dead Father.

I'm sure you don't mind, said Thomas. Doubtless you have others just as sumptuous.

He handed the buckleless belt back to the Dead Father.

I don't mind?

Do you mind?

Yes, Julie asked interestedly, do you mind?

I was always rather fond of that one.

Surely you have others just as fine.

Yes I have a great many belt buckles.

I am delighted to hear it.

Not here. Not with me, the Dead Father said.

You can have my old belt buckle, Thomas said. It will do.

Yes, Julie said, it will do.

Quite a good buckle, my old buckle, Thomas said.

Thank you, said the Dead Father, accepting the old buckle.

Not as fine as your former belt buckle, of course.

It isn't, the Dead Father said. I can see that.

That's why I wanted yours, Thomas explained.

I understand that, said the Dead Father. You wanted the better buckle.

And now I have it, said Thomas.

He patted himself on the belt buckle.

47

Looks quite good I think.

It does, said Julie.

Yes, Emma agreed.

Gives you a bit more dash, said Julie. More dash than you had before.

Thank you, Thomas said. And to the Dead Father: And thank *you*.

My pleasure, said the Dead Father. Good to be able to do something for you younger men, once in a while. Good to be able to *give*. Giving is, in a sense—

No, said Thomas, let us be clear. You didn't give. I took. There is a difference. I took it away from you. Just get it straight. The matter's trivial, but I want no misunderstanding. *I took it. Away* from *you*.

Oh, said the Dead Father.

He thought for a moment.

Will there be consolation?

Yes, said Thomas. You may make a speech.

No, Julie said. No speech.

A speech to the men? asked the Dead Father. To my assembled loyal, faithful—

No, said Julie.

Yes, said Thomas. Tomorrow.

Tomorrow?

Maybe tomorrow, said Thomas.

My speech!

To bed, said Thomas. All to bed now. Pleasant dreams.

Thomas regarded his orange tights, his orange boots, his new silver belt buckle.

Yes! he said.

7

Let him make his speech, Julie said.

Yesterday you said no.

I was in a fouler mood yesterday. Today I am in a fairer mood.

That's interesting, Thomas said. How do you do that?

I ignore sense data, she said, let him make his speech.

Thomas turned to the Dead Father.

Would you like to make your speech now?

I have prepared some remarks, said the Dead Father. Remarks which are perhaps not without pertinency.

Thomas gathered together the men and Emma.

The men stood in a ragged half circle. The nineteen. Edmund with his hand on his back pocket, where the flask was. Emma at one tip of the crescent, Julie at the other.

The Dead Father stepped forward and assumed his speaking position, a kind of forwardly lean.

All the men lighted cigarettes. Julie lighted a cigarette as did Emma.

The Dead Father placed the tips of the fingers of his two hands together.

In considering, he said, inconsidering inconsidering inconsidering the additionally arriving human beings annually additionally arriving human beings each producing upon its head one hundred thousand individual hairs some retained and some discarded—

All the men sat down and began talking to each other.

In contemplating I say these additionally arrived human beings not provided for by anticipatory design hocus or pocus and thus problematical, we must reliably extend a set of ever-advancing speeding poised lingering or dwelling pattern behaviors sufficient unto the day or adequate until the next time. Given the existence of the next time, anticipatory design neurosis designs for integration of the until-then-threatening non-self-requested experience of life and sweet, sweet variable stresses and flows to carry inward and inwardize if rain floods fires earthquakes tornadoes do not occur as predicted but look out of the window and see how dark the sky, how bold the wind, how whipped the trees, how gravitational the red falling skinripping rooftiles not provided for by anticipatory design fury preallotted to the discontinuance of consciousness known as sleep, let us pray. Tensionally cohered universe here today and gone tomorrow finity inward and finity outward and ever-advancing speeding poised lingering or dwelling particles in waveful duality and progressive conceptioning and Father's Day interface with holistic behaviors unpredicted by parts such as you, me, them, and we, and I, and he, and she, and it. These, assigned by a static or "at rest" analysis to super series of unpredictable mathematical frequencies composed of complementary and reciprocal numbers found in cyclic bundling of experience not necessarily compromised by variable geographic bundle limitations, but sometimes, as in the song at twilight when the lights are low and the flickering shadows softly come and go, to multidynamically blossom or burst forth in beauty or pain and pre- and postnatal . . . disappointments . . . next appropriate trial balance struck . . . as to what might be . . . in the best case . . . however. However. Given the already-secreted true experience of the regeneratively-evolving comprehensive world-design effort against fire flood pestilence violent atmospheric disturbance and providing seventeen cubic feet of air per minute per person free of toxic or disagreeable odors or dust, or malice, we feel that metals broadly speaking and synthetics narrowly speaking will interlink into continuously improving world-around extra-corporeal networks, networks within which only individual man presents himself as an inherent island of physical discontinuity sad to say, sad to say, physical discontinuity and torpor, total velocities of which known practices have proved inadequate to solve. Given however all-over compensatory design despair such as is known to you and known to me, and freakiness, and bearing in mind push-pull as prior to and above all, and disregarding those whose larger pattern security is challenged or threatened by these systematically pulsing alternations, we project your existence here as possibly tolerable within tolerances of .01, .02, and .03, given uptooling of social engineering extra-genetic razzle postpartum reprepositioning and I spy. Thank you.

The Dead Father waited for the applause.

A storm of applause from the men!

Thank you, the Dead Father said, thank you.

Prolonged and fervent applause. Whistles. Stamping of feet. Waving of handkerchiefs (the women).

Thank you. Thank you.

A wonderful speech, said Thomas.

A marvelous speech, said Julie, would you autograph my program.

Thank you, said the Dead Father, of course.

Quite extraordinary, said Emma, what did it mean?

Thank you, said the Dead Father, it meant I made a speech.

Beautifully done, said Thomas, are you free for lunch?

Thank you, said the Dead Father, I think so.

Julie was wiping the Dead Father's brow, with her handkerchief.

A long time since I've heard anything like it, she

said, a very long time, not since my student days in fact.

Thank you, said the Dead Father.

The men loved it, said Thomas.

Yes, said the Dead Father.

Positively on the edge of my chair, said Emma, figuratively speaking.

Thank you, said the Dead Father, it was a pisser all right.

Enough! said Julie.

Why is it, asked the Dead Father, that alone among the members of this party I am not allowed to be filthy-mouthed?

Because you are an old fart, she said, and old farts must be notably clean of mouth in order to mitigate the disgustingness of being old farts.

The Dead Father lunged against his cable.

Look how the red is rising to his top, Emma observed.

The Dead Father burst off down the road, his cable trailing.

He is going to do it again, said Thomas.

They followed at a rapid pace.

They found the Dead Father standing in a wood, slaying. First he slew a snowshoe rabbit cleaving it in twain with a single blow and then he slew a spiny anteater and then he slew two rusty numbats and then whirling the great blade round and round his head he slew a wallaby and a lemur and a trio of ouakaris and a spider monkey and a common squid. Then moving up and down the green path in his rage he dispatched a macaque and a gibbon and fourscore innocent chinchillas who had been standing idly by watching the great slaughter. Then he rested standing with the point of his sword stuck in the earth and his two hands folded upon the hilt. Then he again as if taken by a fit set about the bloody work slaying a prairie dog and a beaver and a gopher and a dingo and a honey badger and an otter and a house cat and a tapir and a piglet. Then his anger grew and he called for a

52

brand of even greater weight and length which was brought him by a metaphorically present gillie and seizing it with his two fine-formed and noble hands he raised it above his head, and every living thing within his reach trembled and every dead thing within his reach remembered how it got that way, and the very trees of the wood did seem to shrink and step away. Then the Dead Father slew a warthog and a spotted fawn and a trusting sheep and a young goat and a marmoset and two greyhounds and a draghound. Then, kicking viciously with his noble and shapely foot at the piles of the slain, raw and sticky corpses drenching the earth in blood on every side, he cleared a path to a group of staring pelicans slicing the soft white thin necks of them from the bodies in the wink of an eye. Then he slew a cassowary and a flamingo and a grebe and a heron and a bittern and a pair of ducks and a shouting peacock and a dancing crane and a bustard and a lily-trotter and, wiping the sacred sweat from his brow with one ermine-trimmed sleeve, slew a wood pigeon and a cockatoo and a tawny owl and a snowy owl and a magpie and three jackdaws and a crow and a jay and a dove. Then he called for wine. A silver flagon was brought him and he downed the whole of it in one draught looking the while out of the corner of his ruby eye at a small iguana melted in terror against the limb of a tree. Then he tossed the silver flagon into the arms of a supposititious cupbearer sousing the cupbearer's hypothetical white tunic with the red of the (possible) wine and split the iguana into two halves with the point of his sword as easily as one skilled in the mystery fillets a fish. Then the Dead Father resumed his sword work in earnest slaying divers small animals of every kind, so that the heaps mounted steaming to the right and to the left of him with each passionate step. A toad escaped.

Heavy work, the Dead Father said, looking pleased. See how many!

Thomas was collecting the carcasses of the edible.

See how many! the Dead Father said again.

Truly formidable, Julie said, to please him. Sword play of this quality has not been seen since the days of Frithjof, Lancelot, Paracelsus, Rogero, Artegal, Otuel, Ogier the Dane, Rinaldo, Oliver, Koll the Thrall, Haco I, and the Chevalier Bayard.

Rather good I think, said the Dead Father, for an old man.

His smoking whinyard wiped upon the green grass.

Emma's gaze (admiring).

See how long it is, the Dead Father said, and how limber.

He cut a few figures in the air with it: quinte, sixte, septime.

And now, lunch, Julie said.

She produced from the knapsack a new tablecloth and a new seating plan.

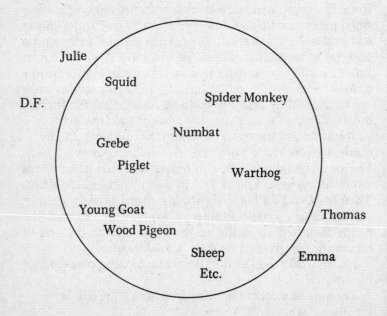

I have been elevated, in the arrangements! the Dead Father exclaimed.

Temporary happiness of the Dead Father.

And I, relegated, Thomas said. He gave Julie a straight look.

Julie returned the straight look.

The Dead Father reached for Julie's bare toe.

Please release my toe.

The Dead Father continued to grasp the toe.

Toe, he said, now there's an interesting word. Toe. Toe. Toe. Toe. Toe. A veiny toe. Red lines on toe. Succulent toe. Succulent, succulent toe. Succulent succulent succulent—

The Dead Father placed the toe in his mouth.

Thomas rapped the Dead Father sharply in the forehead, across the cloth.

Toe fell from the mouth. The Dead Father clutched his forehead.

You have rapped the Father, he said between moans. Again. You *should not* rap the Father. You *must not* rap the Father. You *cannot* rap the Father. Striking the *sacred* and *holy* Father is an offense *of the gravest nature*. Striking the noble, wise, all-giving Dead Father is—

More grebe? Julie asked.

Is there mustard? Thomas asked.

In the pot.

Have the troops fed themselves? Julie asked.

Thomas peered up the road. Cooking fires were visible.

They are eating hearty, he said, because they know what is ahead.

What is ahead? asked the Dead Father.

The Wends, Thomas said.

The Wends? What are they?

They are what is ahead.

What is peculiar about them? the Dead Father asked.

They don't like us.

He lifted his hand and rotated it languidly, representing negligence and of-no-consequence.

Don't like us? Why is that?

First, because we are armed and alien walkers through their domains. Second, because *you* are, in one of your aspects, a gigantic and strange and awe-inspiring object.

I do inspire awe, said the Dead Father. Better than anybody. A lifetime of it. Did I not once rule the Wends?

You did, you did, said Thomas, with an iron hand.

How is it I rule them no longer?

It is because you are slipping into the starry starry night, Julie said, together with all your works and pomps. Rule of the Wends was taken away from you in 1936.

It will be a hot thing, probably, Thomas said. Touch and go.

How many of them are there?

Near to a million, at the last census.

How many of us are there?

Twenty-three, Thomas said. Counting Edmund.

Groan from Julie.

Thomas, said the Dead Father, let us change the subject. We can talk about something interesting, giraffes for example. Or you can explain yourself. It is always interesting to hear someone explaining himself.

Let us talk about giraffes, said Thomas, when I explain myself I tend to stutter. Of course I don't know a great deal about giraffes. They are said to be very intelligent. They have beautiful eyes. They have beautiful eyelashes. Tongues extend to twenty inches. Not much of a mane. Terrific base of the neck. Low fluttering voice. Faster than a horse and can travel longer distances at speed. Can beat lion in fight using hooves unless lion gets lucky. Herds running from twenty to thirty are not uncommon each containing several males but many more females.

Thomas paused.

Only old males are excluded and live in isolation, he said.

I am offended, said the Dead Father. Again.

Then we won't talk about giraffes any more, Thomas

said, I will instead explain myself. I will give you the short form, Thomas said, the basic datatata. I was bbbbbbborn twice-twenty-less-one years ago in a great city the very city in fact from which we have subtracted you. As a new creature on the earth I was of course sent to school where I did reasonably well except where I did reasonably badly. As a child I had the necessary sicknesses seriatim a pox here a measle there broke a bone now and then just to keep in step with the others blacked an eye and had an eye blacked now and then just to keep in step with the others. I then proceeded to higher education as it is called and was educated upon by a team of masked gowned and scrubbed specialists, top performers every one. It had been decided that I would be educated up to the height of two meters and this was done over a pppppperiod of. Next, my convalescence which was spent as was right and proper and natural and good in military service chiefly in far parts and strange climes, learning there how to salute and stamp my foot at the same time in the English wwwwwway, a skill that has been endlessly useful to me ever since. Also a certain amount of truckling, a skill that has been endlessly useful to me ever since. Also how to make friends with the mess sergeant, a skill that et cetera et cetera. Also how to dig a latrine wherein one may spend many happy and productive hours as have we all reading the great Robert Burton. Next, I returned to the educational arena and studied one of the sort-of sciences, sociology to be precise, but quickly learned that I had no talent for it. Nnnnnnext, wishing with all my heart and all my soul to be true to the aspirations and prefabrications of my generation the boys of '34 to be precise, I married. Oh, did I marry. I married and married and married moving from comedy to farce to burlesque with lightsome heart. Oh joy oh bliss oh joy oh bliss. When the bliss had blistered and the smoke had cleared I found that I had fathered, but only once, nota bene nota bene. Then a period of what I can only describe

57

as vacancy. During this period I spent much of my time watching single-engine aircraft practicing stalls and hoping that an engine would fail so that I could see the crash. None ever did. After this I prepared to reenter the mainscream of commercial life. Superbly equipped as I was for nothing-in-particular, I fitted myself into the slot "Navaho lawgiver" but this was a flop because first I am not a Navaho and second there are as you know no Navahos in our country. Pity. I was rather good at chanting. Then I did a bit of poaching. Poached trout from government hatcheries, mostly, sorry disestimable work which dddddid nothing to raise the low esteem in which the organism held itself. I was back where I had started, in low esteem. I then spent some several years in a monastery, but was ejected for consuming too much of the product, a very fine cognac. Then I began to read philosophy.

And what did philosophy teach you? asked the Dead Father.

It taught me that I had no talent for philosophy, said Thomas, bbbbbbut—

But what?

But I think everyone should have a little philosophy, Thomas said. It helps, a little. It helps. It is good. It is about half as good as music.

8

A meeting. The men discontent. Crowded around Thomas. His orange tights, orange boots, silver belt buckle with rubies, white Sabatini shirt. His clear and true gold-rimmed spectacles. Complaints of the men: (1) Quality of the pemmican (2) That the leadership better fed, in general, than the rank and file (3) That the cable was cutting into shoulders and where were promised heavy canvas gloves? (4) Edmund (5) The rum ration could be doubled without damaging the high regard in which the rank and file held the leadership (6) What plan for dealing with possibly hostile Wends? (7) Attention of the women monopolized by the leadership (8) Edmund (9) Couldn't the women just come and talk to them sometimes? (10) That the Dead Father sometimes dead weight, sometimes live weight, variations made feasance more difficult than strictly necessary, see contract provisions D, E, and F (11) Truncation of the pornographic film and what had happened next? (12) What of wholly arbitrary and ill-considered ban on fraternization with locals in territories hayfooted/strawfooted through? (13) Nonexistence of chaplain (14) Happy birthday. It is my birthday? Thomas exclaims, astonished. Yes, men reply, today's the day, where is the party? Thomas counting on his fingers. The men watch. Yes it is my birthday, he says at length, God damn it, you are right as rain. General heehaw, battering of Thomas's back, Edmund whisks flask from hip, tilts. The Dead Father sitting in the road looking off into the far distance where fields of garlic grow. Thomas removes flask from Edmund's mouth. Julie practicing harmonica, tune "Oh, Give Me a Home Where the Buffalo Roam." Emma gazing at immense shoulder of Dead Father, speculatively. Thomas begins to answer complaints point by point. Pemmican good for you, he says. Etc. Julie puts away mouth organ, moves to side of Emma.

Give you a shirtful of sore tit.

Give you a fret in the gizzard.

I tried to tell you but you wouldn't listen.

Think I'm getting nosebleed.

Ways of dealing with them when they don't want you.

Friendship is difficult at best.

People are frightened.

They disagree with me regularly but are not disloyal to me.

Said there were various ways of handling it but I thought I could keep the lid on.

Wake up one dark night with a thumb in your eye.

Strung out like that along the hedges.

Colder weather coming and then warmer.

Since you have not as yet responded to my suggestion.

Matter of paring down to a supportable minimum.

Throw a little shit into the game.

Always darkest just before the dawn.

Take it any way you like it.

Stop being petty, stop trying to cut each other's throat.

If I pop one will you pop one?

I mean when you're feeling bad you're glad to be alive.

What is the motivation?

I can't remember.

At other times unconscious in the street.

How did that make you feel?

Intolerably angry for short periods.

Feeling is what's important.

You can lose confidence in your own experiences.

Various circumstances requiring my attention.

Something trembling in the balance.

Where can a body get a hit around here?

It's all been carefully considered.

Have you tried any of the others?

I just see whether they're friendly or unfriendly.

A week later she applied for a post in Warsaw.

As a wet nurse.

Yes, as a wet nurse. She was accepted.

They like to suck.

They do like to suck.

Worn out your welcome.

Getting very fond of you and your hands.

That's my business.

He's not bad-looking.

It's no mystery.

Why hasn't anyone had the simple decency?

It's perfectly obvious.

Probably we should have spoken up before this.

That's one way of looking at it.

Unable to take him seriously at any level.

Where can a body get a spritz around here?

That's my business.

If I pull this little white string, will you explode?

That's my business.

Then he sobs, and faints.

Does it hurt?

I can make it hot for you.

Learning to put the world together.

The white vase holding the marigolds had fallen to the floor.

The bathtub proved impossible to smash although I tried.

God knows you tried.

God knows I tried.

Dark hair across the pillow.
I can do anything when it's not important.
Very busy making the arrangements.
Will it hurt?
Large piece of white plaster fell off the wall then.
What were we eating?
Cold rolled veal.
Did we have a good time?
Scrumptious.
Will it rain again again?
Something is wrong.
You must have studied English.
The waiter was listening.
Like trying to digest a saddle.
Wake up one dark night with a kiss in your eye.
That was in Barcelona. Rounded up as a work-shy element.
Much cry and little wool.
Ready again to send his Son to die for us.
Like sending a hired substitute to the war.
I rehearsed the argument with him.
Until the scaring bell rang.
What?
Until the scaring bell rang.
What?
Spiritual aridity which was quite hard to reconcile with his surface gaiety.
In a symbiotic hug resembling that which obtains between pigeons and old ladies with bread crumbs.
Did you find the scene disgusting?
I'm not into disgust.
Thought I heard a dog barking.
Reels of 16-mm. film each with a photograph on the box suggesting the particular motif or specialty.
Until the scaring bell rang.
What?
Remembering, leaving, returning, staying.

Two is one too many.

Slept with a man once it was a very pleasant experience.

Where the buffalo roam.

In a bed.

Time to go.

No it's not.

Hair on it.

No it hasn't.

Have you tried any of the others?

Haven't made up my mind.

Dog-Whipping Day. Eighteenth of October.

I tried to tell you but you wouldn't listen.

What?

Simple, honest, generous feelings.

That's one way of looking at it.

Self-respect.

Yes I've had self-respect.

Yes I've had self-respect too it's a very good thing self-respect.

Yes I've had self-respect for a very long time.

Yes I've had it for a very long time too.

Yes I can take it or leave it.

Yes once you've had it for a very long time it doesn't make much difference any more.

You questioning my value system?

Not me.

You questioning what I swear by?

Not me I don't give a rat's ass.

A little forest or a night of dancing.

You can bank on it.

Perhaps it's medical.

Sometimes he smells medical.

Nobody ever died of it.

I've heard that.

Elegant way of putting chairs here and there.

A lady always does.

Any artist will do.
Chewing red candy hearts.
And the myriad flower stalls with their bursting . . .
sun-dapple . . . of the rainbow . . . good God.
I read about it. In *Die Welt*.

9

I wouldn't mind a drink right now, said the Dead Father. Some little something.

I could stand a drink, said Julie.

Remember the last time you had a drink, Thomas said to her.

Oh boy, she said. Yep. Sure do.

Cobwebs in my throat, said Emma.

The men look like they need a drink, said the Dead Father, shading his eyes with one hand and peering up the road.

Well, God damn it, I guess we'd better have a drink, then, said Thomas.

He signaled the men to halt. The cable loose in the road.

Julie broke out the whiskey.

What is it today? asked the Dead Father.

Aquavit with a beer chaser, she said.

Wow, said Emma, tasting her glass. Wow wow wow wow.

Yes, Julie said. It's giggles in the sphinxeries.

Quite good, said Thomas, the beer helps.

I like this drink, Emma said, this is good stuff, can I have two more?

One more, said Thomas, we have many a league to cover yet this day.

You are being stuffy. I find that quite extraordinary. You of all people.

What does that mean? Thomas asked. Me of all people?

Why are you always telling everybody what to do?

I *like* telling everybody what to do, Thomas said. It is a great pleasure, being boss. One of the greatest. Wouldn't you agree? he said to the Dead Father.

It is one of the best pleasures, the Dead Father said. No doubt about it. It is bang-up, but mostly we don't let people know. Mostly we downplay the pleasure. Mostly we stress the anguish. We keep the pleasure to ourselves, in our hearts. Occasionally we may show a bit of it to someone—lift a corner of the veil, as it were. But we only do that in order to certify the pleasure to ourselves. Full disclosure is almost unheard of. Thomas is being criminally frank, in my opinion.

Emma threw down a guzzle of beer, then a guzzle of aquavit.

Okay Fat Daddy, she said, show me how to dance.

What? said the Dead Father.

Emma wearing blue velvet pants burnished to silver where she sits.

Do you know the Hucklebuck?

I do not.

Emma begins to demonstrate. Parts of Emma hucklebuckling in various directions.

Amazing, said the Dead Father. I remember.

Julie and Thomas watching.

It is obvious that but for a twist of fate I would be his and not yours, Julie said. Had I lived within his domains at a time when he was administering them with full heaviness of hand—

He was a goat, Thomas said, that's well known.

Goatish still. Cops a feel whenever he can.

I've noticed.

Prefers the bum, she said, a great grab he's got there.

I've observed.

And in terms of verbal rather than physical attentions, he has proposed variously a shake of the sheets, a dive in the dark, a leap up the ladder, and a goose-and-duck.

And you replied?

With harrowing sweetness, as usual. Still he has something.

Oh yes, Thomas said, he has something. I would not dream of denying it.

Authority. Fragile, yet present. He is like a bubble you do not wish to burst.

But remember there was a time when he was slicing people's ears off with a wood chisel. Two-inch blade. And remember there was a time when his voice, his plain unamplified voice, could turn your head inside out.

Hunkwash, she said, you are perpetuating myths.

The hell I am, Thomas said. It happened.

You don't appear to me to be overly hurt or damaged.

There are some times when you are not too bright, said Thomas.

Times when I am not too what?

Bright, said Thomas, there are some times when you are not too bright.

Well fuck you, she said.

Well fuck *you,* Thomas said, there are some times when I forget and tell the truth.

Sloppy, sloppy, she said. Self-pity monstrously unattractive.

Oh well damn well yes. I'm sorry. But I am taking action, am I not? I could as well have sat at home, worn the cap-and-bells and bought lottery tickets hoping for the twist-of-fate that would change my life.

Me, she said. Me, me.

There is that.

You and I, she said, reaching into her knapsack for a bit of bhang. Have a chew?

Not now, thanks.

You and I, she said, the two of us.

Thomas began counting on his fingers.

Yes, he said.

And Emma, she said. I've seen you looking at her.

I look at everything, Thomas said. Everything that is in front of me. Emma is in front of me. Therefore I look at Emma.

And she at you, Julie said, I've seen some gazes.

She's not bad-looking, Thomas said.

But we, you and I, care for each other, Julie said. It is a fact.

A temporary fact, said Thomas.

Temporary!

Expectoration of bhang juice (emphatic).

My God, I'm simply telling the truth, said Thomas.

Viper, she said.

I know no better soul, he said, and the body is also attractive.

Measuring, are you? A measuring man.

Julie cramming more hemp into her mouth.

You forget the decay of time, Thomas said, I never forget it.

I don't like it.

Who likes it?

I put out of mind that which is injurious to mind. You revel in it.

I do not revel in it.

The two of us, she said, damn it, can't you get this simple idea into your head? The two of us against the is.

Temporarily, said Thomas.

Oh you are a viper.

A student of decay, is all.

Julie began to unbutton her shirt.

Yes, that's a way, said Thomas. Fifteen minutes or in the best case, thirty-five.

Come crawl behind a bush with me.

With all my heart, said Thomas, but I cannot abandon what I know. One doesn't find an absolute every day.

You are an apprentice fool, she said, not even a full fool, nevertheless I will give you a little taste, because I like you. You are a lucky dog.

Thomas spoke a long paragraph to the effect that this was true.

Julie pulling at Thomas's sleeve.

Thomas and Julie underneath the bush. Thomas holding Julie's feet in his hands.

Wash feet, he said.

Yes now that you mention it, she said.

I will wash them for you if you wish.

Not necessary. I know the drill.

Washcloth, he said. That's the little blue square one.

Right.

Rough-textured.

I've seen it.

Usually damp.

I remember.

I could just put some bags on them I suppose, heavy canvas bags with locks like the Mail Department uses.

Oh misery me.

The backs of the knees are on the other hand positively lustrous.

Not too bad are they?

Nine lines and a freckle, all immaculate. Nothing to be desired. The height of.

Could an Emma do as well?

I don't know, said Thomas. I'll have to think about it.

Julie made a circle of thumb and forefinger and popped him smartly on the ball.

Anguish of Thomas.

It will pass, she said, dearly beloved, it is only temporary.

69

10

Edmund talking to Emma. Beam of Emma. Washing of
socks in the small stream. Discussion of foot care (general). Thomas seated on the ground, back supported by
tree, smoking, contemplative. Edmund telling Emma
that, all things considered, she is the best. Beam of
Emma. Julie and the Dead Father holding hands. Thomas
smoking. The men playing whist, quoits, boccie. Terrain
features being cut down to feed the fires. All the men
wearing dark-blue suits with ties. Edmund wearing dark-
blue suit with tie. Thomas wearing dark-blue suit with
tie. The Dead Father wearing dark-blue suit with tie.
Bending over spits rotating with spitted small animals.
Edmund tapped on the cheek with Emma's fan. God Almighty. Emma tapped on the cheek with Edmund's
thumb. God Almighty. Emma tells Edmund that he
doesn't understand. Thumb not to tap cheeks with, she
says. Thumb not gracile but rather stumpy, fat, she says.
Index finger better if cheek is to be tapped and fan not
available. Edmund fucks everything up, she says. Poor
wooer, she says. May consider himself as having status
of least-favored-nation, wooing-wise. Crushed Edmund.
Edmund falls into flask. Thomas turns head, notices dis-
tress of Edmund. Thomas does nothing. Julie looks at
Thomas and notices him doing nothing. Julie says to the
Dead Father: Sometimes best to do nothing. The Dead

Father replies: Maybe mostly. They continue to hold hands and the Dead Father also gropes a bare foot with the hand that is not holding hands. Julie retracts foot. Thomas smokes. Events in the sky. Starfall scattering in the dark part. Clouds moving implacably (left to right) offstage, toward the wings. Thomas smoking. The Dead Father attempting to insert hand (left) between waistband of Julie's skirt and Julie. Repulsed (warmly). Julie takes the Dead Father's watch fob and places it in her pocket. The Dead Father smiles. A gift, he says, for you. Thank you, Julie says, thank you thank you. Thank me, says the Dead Father, I am used to it. I do thank you, Julie says, and your shoe buckles are nice too. They are nice, says the Dead Father, that is why I have them there, on my shoes, because they are nice. Both regard the Dead Father's silver shoe buckles. Thomas smoking. Edmund with most of his mouth around the mouth of the flask. Emma interviewing the men. How high are they? 6'1", 5'11", 4'2", and so forth. For my files, Emma says. Thomas smoking, scratches upper left cheekbone lightly with free fingers of left hand. Alarm arrives from the outpost. Alexander runs to Thomas. Whispers to Thomas. Thomas extinguishes cigar, rises, looks about for his sword. Finds same, buckles on sword belt, tucks orange tight (right) into top of orange boot.

The Wends are here, he said.

They hurried to the spot.

The road blockaded. The path barred. An army deployed across the way and far far up on every piece of high ground available.

Well now, said the chief Wend, aren't you a pretty sight.

Good day, Thomas said.

Julie lit a cigarette as did Emma.

Well now, the chief Wend said again, do you intend traveling more along this road?

With your permission.

Would you be hauling that great ugly thing there through the length and breadth of the country of the Wends?

Only the length, said Thomas. Not the breadth.

We don't want him, the chief Wend said. No thank you.

We hadn't in mind leaving him, said Thomas. Just passing through.

Is it what I think it is? the Wend asked.

It is the Dead Father.

That's what I thought. That's what I thought. About three thousand cubits, I'd estimate.

Thirty-two hundred.

How do you get him around bends in the road?

He is articulated.

No rigor mortis?

None.

Then he is not properly dead.

In a sense.

Has it both ways does he?

In this as in everything.

Is there an odor?

The odor of sanctimony, is all.

Excreta?

Monstrous of course.

Does he molest women?

Not exactly.

What does that mean, "not exactly"?

He tries but I restrain him.

How is that done?

Rap to the forebrain.

Does he converse and issue dicta?

Thomas did not answer.

Well, does he?

Nothing that cannot be enthusiastically ignored.

The Wend chieftain sat down in the middle of the road, cross-legged.

Tarry a bit, he said.

They sat. The nineteen. Emma. Julie. Thomas. The Dead Father.

Then the Wend army sat with a noise like land sliding.

Let me tell you about the Wends, the Wend said. We Wends are not like other people. We Wends are the fathers of ourselves.

You are?

Yes, said the Wend, that which all men have wished to be, from the very beginning, we are.

Amazing, said Thomas, how is that accomplished?

It is accomplished by being a Wend, the leader said. Wends have no wives, they have only mothers. Each Wend impregnates his own mother and thus fathers himself. We are all married to our mothers, in proper legal fashion.

Thomas was counting on his fingers.

You are skeptical, said the chief. That is because you are not a Wend.

The mechanics of the thing elude me, said Thomas.

Take my word for it, said the Wend, it is not more difficult than Christianity. The point is, we are not used to having flaming great fathers about to pick at and badger us. We haven't the taste for it. In fact, we are violently prejudiced against it. Therefore this huge big carcass of yours is not something we care to have within our country, even briefly. Some of him might rub off.

Is there another road? asked Thomas.

None, said the Wend, that will get you where you are aiming. I take it you seek the Fleece.

That is correct, said Thomas.

We are not sure it exists, said the Wend.

It exists, Thomas said. In a sense.

I see, said the Wend. Well, *if* it exists, it lies on the other side of the country of the Wends.

A problem, said Thomas.

You could of course fight your way through, the Wend suggested.

Thomas regarded the Wend army, in its thousands.

This is just the Third Armored, the chief said, indicating his mailed and belted followers. The First Armored is way back over to the east. The Ninth Hoplites are over to the west. The Twenty-sixth Impi is in a blocking position, I can't tell you where. These are just the border troops. They would be delighted, were you to decide to fight your way through.

We are three-and-twenty, Thomas said. Counting Edmund.

Your mothers are quite beautiful, said the chieftain. Those two there, the light one and the dark-haired one. Very lovely.

They are not mothers, Thomas said.

Probably they could learn very quickly, said the Wend, motherhood comes naturally to most.

What if he were just a little more dead? Thomas asked, indicating the Dead Father. Would he then be transportable through the country of the Wends?

Well of course if he were cut up and cooked, that would put quite a different face on the matter, the chieftain said. Then we could be sure.

Further than I'm prepared to go, said Thomas.

Meet you halfway, said the Wend, just boil him for a day and we'll give you free passage.

Not a pot big enough in the wide world, said Thomas. May I suggest this: We'll whack off a leg and barbecue same as an earnest of good faith and token of guaranteed non-contaminaciousness.

A leg? said the Wend.

He pondered for a moment.

That should be sufficient. But you'll be closely watched, now. No hanky-panky.

As closely as you like, said Thomas, but I can't be held responsible for the stench.

The chief Wend returned to his men. Thomas ordering wood gathered for the great fire.

What's this? asked the Dead Father. What now?

A little tableau, said Thomas, you have the best part, lie down, close eyes, howl on cue, and stay stiff as a board after.

Why? asked the Dead Father.

Why me no whys, said Thomas, quickly, stretch out.

The Dead Father lay down in the road, the whole great length of him.

Anxiety of Emma, Julie, Edmund, Alexander, Sam.

The men return with great bundles of firewood.

Thomas drew his sword and approached the left leg, the leg mechanical, not human. He began to whack.

11

The road. The caravan. People taking pictures of the caravan with little pronghorn cameras. Flashes of light.

My leg is black, said the Dead Father.

But functioning, said Thomas, congratulate yourself.

You carved me very neatly, said the Dead Father. I admit it.

Oh it was a grand fire, said Thomas, very persuasive.

The Wend country is bumpy to a fault, said the Dead Father. I am glad we are out of it.

Jumble-gut lane, Thomas agreed.

Those that are the fathers of themselves miss something, said the Dead Father. Fathers, to be precise.

Fatherhood as a substructure of the war of all against all, said Thomas, we could discuss that.

I can speak to that, said Julie.

Me too, said Emma, for I know nothing about it, and am thus presuppositionless.

A state of grace, philosophically, the Dead Father observed.

Julie began.

The father is a motherfucker, she said.

By definition, said Thomas.

The vagina, she said, is not where it's at.

We agree, said Thomas, we've heard that.

Moving north, one finds a little button.

Nods of comprehension.

Now it does no good to *mash down* on the button. It's not an elevator button, it's not a doorbell. The button should not be mashed down on. It should be—

She stopped for a word.

Celebrated, suggested Thomas.

Titivated, suggested Emma.

No mashing down! Julie said fiercely.

Nods of accord.

The phallus, she continued, is next to useless for the purpose. Rolling pins should never be employed. Streams of blue blood—

What has this to do with fatherhood? asked the Dead Father.

I talk about what I want to talk about, said Julie, this is a digression.

Indeed.

The fucked mother conceives, Julie said. The whelpling is, after agonies I shall not describe, whelped. Then the dialogue begins. The father speaks to it. The "it" in a paroxysm of not understanding. The "it" whirling as in a centrifuge. Looking for something to tie to. Like a boat in a storm. What is there? The father.

Where is the mother? asked Emma.

The mother hath not the postlike quality of the father. She is more like a grime.

A grime?

Overall presence distributed in discrete small black particles all over everything, said Julie.

Post and grime, said the Dead Father. You do have a dismal view of things.

Where did I learn it? For the mind of me to have formulated these formulations, must they not have a grounding in external reality? I am not just idly—

Are you about to cry? asked the Dead Father.

No, said Julie, I never cry. Except when I realize what I have done.

77

Who speaks for the father? asked the Dead Father. Who in God's name—

The family unit produces zombies, psychotics, and warps, Thomas said. In excess of what is needed.

Eighteen percent at the last census, Julie added.

I am not saying that it is your fault, he said to the Dead Father.

Edmund would be an example, Emma suggested. Though lovable.

I think not, said Thomas, he is an alkie, is all.

What is he doing now?

Thomas looked up the road.

Sucking on his flask, he said, I have flang three of them into the brush but he always produces another.

Conduct a shakedown, suggested the Dead Father. Stand by your bunks and open your footlockers.

Prefer not to, said Thomas.

Fifty-year-old boys, Julie said, that's another thing.

Are you blaming me? asked the Dead Father.

They exist, said Julie, grinning in their business suits and knickers. And Keds.

What is the cause? asked the Dead Father.

Does he really want to hear the answer? asked Thomas. No. I don't think so. If I were he, I would not want to hear the answer.

They are boys because they don't want to be old farts, said Julie. The old fart is not cherished in this society.

Or old poop, said Thomas, that is another thing they don't want to be.

This language is not very flattering, said the Dead Father. To a man of a certain age.

Stumbling from the stage is anathema to them, said Julie, they want to be nuzzling new women when they are ninety.

What is wrong with that? asked the Dead Father. Seems perfectly reasonable to me.

The women object, she said. Violently.

Emma was peering down the road.

Edmund has fallen flat on his mush in the roadway, she said.

Thomas trotted to the place where the others were picking Edmund up. He returned holding a silver flask.

What's in it? Julie asked.

Thomas tilted the flask.

Anisette, he said, or something sweet.

And furthermore, Julie said to the Dead Father, it is unseemly. Ugly. Nasty-looking, would be a way of putting it.

The Dead Father slipped his cable and stormed off down the road.

He is going to do it again, said Emma. Paint the floor red with blood.

No, said Thomas. He is not.

Thomas caught the Dead Father in two bounds.

Your sword, sir.

My sword?

Surrender your sword. Your maulsticker.

You were being castigatorious, said the Dead Father. Again.

The men watching. Julie and Emma watching.

The sword, said Thomas.

You are asking me to give up my sword?

I am.

Then I shall be swordless. Think what that means.

I have. Long and hard.

Must I?

You must.

The Dead Father unsheathed his sword and gazed at it.

Old Stream-of-Anguish! Companion of my finest hours!

He gazed at Thomas.

Thomas holding out his hand.

He surrendered the sword.

12

The Dead Father plodding along, at the end of his cable. His long golden robes. His long gray hair to the shoulder. His broad and noble brow.

Awfully calm, said Julie.

Placid as a mailman, Thomas agreed, he is trying to be good.

Harder for him than for thee or me, he's not used to it.

I was never good, until I attained my majority, Thomas said. And even then—

I never bothered my pretty head about it, Julie said. Sometimes I did the right thing and sometimes I did the wrong thing. In difficult cases, I shut my eyes and leaped. A great deal of leaping.

And yet in those instances that have feelings attached—

I go against them, she said. My feelings. Method of the utmost trustworthiness, learned from the Carmelites.

I follow my feelings, Thomas said, when I can find them.

He's been very quiet.

Not a peep out of him these many miles.

Has he perhaps twigged?

Look on the bright side, Thomas said, and decide that he has not. It's essential.

A grimace from Julie.

The world's slow stain. Who said that? Preserved from the contagion of, I think, the world's slow stain.

I block on it if I ever knew, Thomas said.

Julie bit off a chew of bhang.

And the men, said Thomas. Some possibility of trouble there.

Nonsense. The men will be adequately recompensed by the reds and blues and silver streaks we have introduced into the gray tusche of their lives. Don't worry about the men. They are only men after all—a tractor could have done the job as well.

The composition would have suffered, Thomas said. Think of it: Up there, the nineteen, the Old Incorrigibles, hauling upon the cable. The line of the cable itself, taut, angled, running from there to here. Finally, the object hauled: the Father, in his majesty. His grandeur. A tractor would have been très insipide.

Chewing of bhang (noncommittal).

Before attaining your majority, Thomas asked, what did you do?

Schemed, mostly. Scheming away night and day, toward the achievement of ends. I woke up angry one morning and stayed angry for years—that was my adolescence. Anger and scheming. How to get out. How to get Lucius. How to get Mark. How to get away from Fred. How to seize power. That sort of thing. And a great deal of care-of-the-body. It was young. It was beautiful. It deserved care.

Is beautiful, Thomas said. Is beautiful, beloved.

Thank you, she said. There were many men, I don't deny it, it was moths to the flame. I tried to love them. Damned difficult. Kept a harpoon gun in my tall window. Tracked them as they moved down the street, in their ridiculous dignity. I never fired although I could have, it was operable. Having them in my sights was enough. My finger on the trigger, always about to go off but never quite. Tension of the most exquisite sort.

I thought it was an objet d'art, Thomas said.

Julie smiled.

Often, when I was young, last year, I walked out to the water. It spoke to me of myself. Images came to me, from the water. Pictures. Large green lawns. A great house with pillars, but the lawns so vast that the house can be seen only dimly, from where we are standing. I am wearing a long skirt to the ground, in the company of others. I am witty. They laugh. I am also wise. They ponder. Gestures of infinite grace. They appreciate. For the finale, I save a life. Leap into the water all clothed and grasping the drowner by the hair, or using the cross-chest carry, get the silly bastard to shore. Have to bash him once in the mush to end his wild panicked struggles. Drag him to the old weathered dock and there, he supine, I rampant, manage the resuscitation. Stand back, I say to the crowd, stand back. The dazed creature's eyes open—no, they close again—no, they open again. Someone throws a blanket over my damp, glistening white, incredibly beautiful shoulders. I whip out my harmonica and give them two fast choruses of "Red Devil Rag." Standing ovation. The triumph is complete.

You left out Albert Schweitzer, Thomas said.

Hard to patch him in, said Julie, but he is there.

At that moment the Dead Father approached Thomas, holding a small box.

A present, he said, for you.

Thank you, said Thomas, what is it?

Open it, said the Dead Father. Open the box.

Thomas opened the box and found a knife.

Thank you, he said, what is it for?

Use it, said the Dead Father. Cut something. Cut something off.

I spoke too soon, Thomas said, he is not reconciled.

I will never be reconciled, the Dead Father said, never. When I am offended, I award punishment. Punishment is a thing I'm good at. I have some rather fine ones. For anyone who dares trifle. On the first day the trifler is well wrapped with strong cords and hung upside down from a flagpole at a height of twenty stories. On the second day the trifler is turned right side up and rehung from the same staff, so as to empty the blood from his head and prepare him for the third day. On the third day the trifler is unwrapped and waited upon by a licensed D.D.S. who extracts every other tooth from the top row and every other tooth from the bottom row, the extractions to be mismatching according to the blueprint supplied. On the fourth day the trifler is given hard things to eat. On the fifth day the trifler is comforted with soft fine garments and flagons and the attentions of lithesome women so as to make the shock of the sixth day the more severe. On the sixth day the trifler is confined alone in a small room with the music of Karlheinz Stockhausen. On the seventh day the trifler is pricked with nettles. On the eighth the trifler is slid naked down a thousand-foot razor blade to the music of Karlheinz Stockhausen. On the ninth day the trifler is sewn together by children. On the tenth day the trifler is confined alone in a small room with the works of Teilhard de Chardin and the music of Karlheinz Stockhausen. On the eleventh day the trifler's stitches are removed by children wearing catcher's mitts on their right and left hands. On the twelfth day—

I apologize for saying you were perpetuating myths, Julie said to Thomas. I am beginning to come round to your opinion.

13

The mountain. The cathedral. The stone steps. Music. Looking down. The windows, apertures. Rows of seated people. The altars, lights, singing. Egg-shaped apertures like seats opening onto the void. The drop. The clouds. Slipping in the seat. Thomas slipping in the seat. Toward the void. Brace foot against edge. Lean back hooking shoulder around opening. Out strolling on the grounds. Flowers blue with a border of white. The Dead Father strolling. Julie strolling. Others strolling. Edmund strolling. The music, a Kyrie. The edge. The fall. Stone steps. Mandrills staring. Photographers and cooks. Thomas sitting in the sloping seat. Slipping toward the edge. Braces foot against the outer wall, which trembles. Hooks shoulder around inner wall and grasps with left hand. Out strolling. Julie speaking to the Dead Father. The Dead Father smiling. People sitting on stone benches. Processional. Under a canopy. Golden censers swinging left right left right. Tall old man in golden mitre. Acolytes. Rings with amethysts. The edge. Looking over the edge. Sheer walls. Clouds. Thomas slipping in the seat. Braces right foot against outer wall. A quilt or blanket slipping toward the edge. Shoulder hooked around inner wall. The wall trembling. The alcove shaped like an egg. Quilt slipping toward the edge. Singing. The mountain. A set of stone steps. The cathedral. Bronze doors intricately worked with scenes. Row of grenadiers in shakos. Kneeling. Interior of the egg. Painted brick, white, curving. Rug or quilt of blue and red slipping toward the edge. In the walls of the cathedral. Windows over the edge. Dies irae, dies illa. The Dead Father sitting in the cathedral gardens. Julie sitting at his feet. The Dead Father's head thrown back against the wall. Julie sketching. Edmund standing near the edge. Edmund eating. People climbing the stone steps in pairs. Standing near the edge. Bronze doors opening. Confessionals in rows. Grenadiers. Acolytes two-by-two under the red canopy. Seminarians following, through the doors. Curving white-painted brick but a stone is loose, several. Pressure against the right edge, which trembles. Grasping the inner edge. Trying to wedge shoulder against the rear wall but the rug is sliding toward the edge. Erotic and religious experience. Thomas strolling about the gardens. The Dead Father's head thrown back against walls of the cathedral. Julie sketching. Slipping. Sketching. Slipping.

It is possible to fall here, Julie said.

I feel it, said Thomas.

Very possible to fall, she said, I get a falling feeling.

Are you frightened, beloved? Thomas asked.

He stuck his sword in the ground and put his arms around her.

Arms around me, she said, that is what I like.

Always arms to put around you, always and everywhere, said Thomas.

Move up more under my breasts so that the bottoms of the breasts can rest upon the tops of the arms, said Julie.

Not in front of me, said the Dead Father.

The tops of the brown arms, said Julie.

The whites of the bottoms of the breasts, said Thomas.

They disengaged.

Is that horseman still following? Emma asked.

Still following, Thomas said. Still.

Julie moved to Emma.

Then your bed was taken away from you.

Yes.

A certain butcherliness not inappropriate.

Will you let him see it?

Hard to tell. Dominant tempo of our national life.

Throws you into no-go situations.

Tricycle a bit in the evenings, now.

Spent his time wetting the bottoms of women.

Youth comes to the fore, youth has its hour of glory.

Like a photograph of a photograph.

Probably we should have spoken up before this.

Gray day, gray day.

I was ill, endless series of unpleasant dreams.

Be grateful if you could find the time to see me.

The terrible temptation which was assailing me will now be understood.

Where the buffalo roam.

I had rubbed myself thoroughly with oil and I carried a large flask of whiskey.

Have to be a little bit tougher.

Thought I heard a dog barking.

In wild places far from the heart.

Tiny silvered hairs that I had thought mine alone.

A lady always does.

Told them how Lenin had appeared to her in a dream.

That's your opinion.

Two dozen white roses accompanied by his card.

I read about it in the *Corriere della Sera*.

It's been so long, been so long.

Free to leave at any moment.

Where can a body get a baiser around here?

Attending, departing, arriving, ignoring.

Hoping this will reach you at a favorable moment.

Fish scales, wastepaper.

Inching by dying by.

Not sad or serious.

It was the damnedest thing.
What?
It was the damnedest thing.
What?
Old Danish saying.
What?
Repetition is reality.
I read about it. In *Politikken*.
The care that a bystander is obliged to exert for an accessible encounter extends past civil inattention to the question of how and when he can present himself for official participation.
I read about it. In a book.
Yes. Erving's.
Yes. Slit your nose for you.
Your many kindnesses and especial favor.
Eats his kids they say.
One way to look at it.
Thought I heard a hog barking.
Joyous and without joy.
The bourgeois press told stories.
Faces?
Yes faces.
What?
Faces.
Something about faces.
Always been very interested in faces.
I'm not into that.
Forever and ever and ever and ever.
Also possible to be a damned fool.
I'm not into that.
Don't blame you I was raised in the faith.
What?
I was raised in the faith.
What?
Been so long, so long.

Attending, departing.

He's a drunk. Which one? All of them. Must be a reason for that.

Have you tried any of the others?

Follow a track by night.

What?

Steer by the stars.

Extremely interested in this position.

Make his ear glow.

Fill his brain full of frisks.

Must be a reason for that.

Her charms had made it possible for her to gain a close insight.

Glad to hear it.

This idiot had led a thoroughly disorderly life.

Sorry to hear that.

Covered with butter.

Chocolate butter?

Yes chocolate butter.

It's the urge to confess.

I've heard about it.

It's sunset across the bay.

It's pencil shavings in the wind.

Tried to get a handle on it.

Give you a shot in the kisser.

I can take care of myself.

No you can't.

There'll always be another chance tomorrow.

No there won't.

Want to get better but seem to be getting worse.

That's your opinion.

Constant memory in the making.

That's one way of looking at it.

The whole thing hinges.

I've heard that.

So as not to have to defecate while being accessible to others for talk.

I can understand that.
Now let us briefly review the kinds of.
Been waiting all day.
She was vulgar.
She was?
Very vulgar.
She is?
Yes very vulgar. Vulgar to a fault.
Really?
One of the most vulgar. Most consistently vulgar.
I'm surprised. I didn't know.
The vulgarest. Vulgarity everywhere.
Happy to have been able to spend this time with you.
So fucking vulgar you wouldn't believe it.
It's red sails in the sunset.
It's moons over Miami.
I didn't really mean that really.
I was wrong I realize that now wrong.
Were you raised in the faith?
No.
You weren't raised in the faith?
Yes I mean I was but I busted out.
Vulgarity everywhere.
The wink is a classic device for establishing.
That's true.
I thanked the large black woman and withdrew.
Holding on tight.
That's right. Holding on tight.
Years not unmarked by hideous strains.
I remember.
Wild and free and.
Pray to St. Jude. And Ganesha.
I really didn't mean that really.
Were you raised in the faith?
I was raised partly in and partly out of the faith.
How did that feel?
Foul.

It felt foul?

Yes foul. Foul foul foul.

Being raised in the faith felt foul?

That's what I said you hard of hearing or something?

I think foreplay is the most interesting part.

Yes foreplay is the most interesting part.

Some people like consummation.

I've heard that. But in my opinion foreplay is the most interesting part. It's more interesting.

Haven't thought much about it really I studied English.

Some people like to get it the hell over with.

Yes I've heard that.

Most of it is interesting if you are interested in it.

I've heard that. You must have studied anatomy.

In extenso.

14

Alexander, Sam, and Edmund. Requesting permission to speak.

Of course, said Thomas. What is it?

Well sir, said Alexander, some of the boys have been thinking.

Yes? What is it they have been thinking?

Well sir, said Alexander, the men have a melancholy.

Oh my, said Thomas. Which?

Well sir, I would say it is the pip. Less a sulk than a sourness.

What are the symptoms?

Headache, vertigo, singing in the ears, much waking, fixed eyes, red eyes, high color, hard belly, short and sharp belchings, dry brains, and pain in the left side. Not each man has every symptom. Most have two. Some have three. One has four.

Me, Edmund said.

Did I not double the rum ration? Thomas asked.

You did, sir, you did, and we are grateful. Yet—

Well what is the issue?

Well sir, I was coming to that. The issue, Alexander said, is ethical.

Oh my. Local or general?

Well sir, we feel maybe we ought not to be doin' what we are doin'. We feel it's a scotomizing, you might say.

91

A what?

A darkening of the truth.

What truth and how darkened?

Well sir, Alexander said, look at it this way. It is this: The grand Father's bein' all hauly-mauly by the likes of us over bump and bumbust and all raggletailed and his poor bumleg all hurty and his grand aura all tarnagled and June bein' a bad month for new enterprises and a bad month for old enterprises accordin' to the starcharts and like that, we that is to say us the men have a faint intustition that maybe the best is not to come in terms of the grand Father the moon-hanger the eye-in-the-sky the old meister the bey window the bit chammer the gaek-warder the incaling the khando kid the neatzam the shot-gun of kyotowing the principal stadtholder the voivode the top wali, this Being, I say, being a Being of the highest anthropocentrictrac interest, as well as the one who keeps the corn popping from the fine green fields and the like and the like, is maybe being abruised and lese-majestied by us poor galoots over many meters of hard cheese days in and out but even a galoot has a brain to wonder with and what we wonder is to what end? for what purpose? are we right? are we wrong? are we culpable? to what degree? will there be a trial after? official inquiry? court of condemnation? white paper? have you told him? if you have told him what have you told him? how much of the blame if there is blame is ours? ten percent? twenty per-cent? in excess of that figure? and searching our hearts as we do each morning and evening and also at midday after lunch and after the dishes have been washed, we wonder whither? what for? can the conscience be cog-gled? *are we doing the right thing*? and with all the love and respect we have for you Thomas-the-Tall-Standing and for your wisdom which we do not deny for a moment and for your heart— To put it in the short form, we are dubious.

An occasion. Thomas rising.

Your questions are good ones, he said. Your concern is well founded. I can I think best respond by relating an anecdote. You are familiar I take it with the time Martin Luther attempted to sway Franz Joseph Haydn to his cause. He called Haydn on the telephone and said, "Joe, you're the best. I want you to do a piece for *us*." And Haydn just said, "No way, Marty. No way."

You have got the centuries all wrong and the telephone should not be in there and anyway I do not get the point, said Edmund.

You see! Thomas exclaimed. *There it is!* Things are not simple. Error is always possible, even with the best intentions in the world. People make mistakes. Things are not done right. Right things are not done. There are cases which are not clear. You must be able to tolerate the anxiety. To do otherwise is to jump ship, ethics-wise.

I hate anxiety, Edmund said. He produced a flask and tilted it.

Have some? he asked Thomas.

What is it?

Paint thinner with a little grenadine.

I'll pass thanks, Thomas said.

You have not resolved our dilemma, said Alexander. If you could give us a statement of purpose, no matter how farfetched or improbable . . . Something we could take back to the boys.

We are helping him through a difficult period, Thomas said, that would be a way of putting it.

Then he was struck, as if by a thought.

It is, you might say, a rehearsal.

15

The Dead Father talking to Emma. Pink hazes of the early morning. Vegetation failures visible, blasted sumac, iris, phlox. Dim low hills beyond. The Dead Father in his golden robes. Emma in her green fatigue pants, green fatigue shirt.

Looking very beautiful this morning, the Dead Father said.

Oh am I, said Emma.

You are a very handsome woman, the Dead Father said.

No no, said Emma, just ordinary. Just an ordinary woman. Another among thousands.

Not at all, not at all. Now I have seen in my time many a one.

Yes, Emma said, I believe it.

Some stunning beauties. Some extraordinary ladies. I can distinguish I think between what is ordinary and what is not. You are sui generis one might say.

Hardly that, Emma said. Just another sand dollar on the beach.

No no no, said the Dead Father, really quite remarkable. The bosom, for example.

Yes, said Emma, there are some who've found it adequate.

Adequate! What a word. Why I've not seen its like in twenty years.

Yes, said Emma, there are some who've found it passable.

I would compare it to that of the Aphrodite of Cyrene if you would take off your shirt so I could see it better.

No, said Emma, I do not think that would be right. You will have to content yourself with the rough approximation of the exterior. The shirt trick is Julie's.

I remember a bosom, the Dead Father said. Might be a better bosom than your own. Might be a worse bosom than your own. Although they are all beautiful, bosoms, all beautiful, each in its own way, foolish to talk of "better" and "worse," it's apples and oranges, really.

What bosom is that that you remember?

The lady was a lawyer. Appeared before me in a matter. I was presiding. Case had to do with a homosexual admiral who'd been caught buggering a black gang. A whole black gang. Down there in the engine room 'midst the steam and grease. Some suggestion of coercion. Some suggestion of abuse of rank. And so on and so on. She was representing the admiral, in her robes. I noticed the robes. There is something very sensual about robes. I was transfixed, couldn't keep my eyes off her. There is a certain line, bosom under robe, I can't describe it. Makes one light-headed. She argued very capably, probably the most thoroughly researched brief I've ever read. The government's case on the other hand very sloppily prepared. I found for her. Strictly on the merits. Merits piled on merits. Afterward, a brandy together in my chambers. She said I wasn't as bad as I'd been painted. I said, Oh yes I was. We had a week together on the island of Ahura. The Bee and the Thistle, as I recall. Incomparable. Taught me a lot of law, she did, and I thought I knew it all. Claudia. Married a sky diver, as I recall. One of those people who fall out of airplanes and drop for thousands

95

and thousands of feet waiting for the umbrella to open. Finally it didn't. A Wednesday, as I recall. I gave her a judgeship and she has twice been cited by the Bar Association for excellence beyond the believable. That was Claudia.

And the bosom? What has happened to it?

Growing in wisdom and beauty, still beating with the conviction that the world can be made equitable, I would suppose. One of my best appointments, in retrospect.

Fretfulness of Emma. Adjustment of shirt, etc. Pulling up of pants. Nervous play of fingers about the throat.

I am old, said the Dead Father, old, old, old. That is why you don't want to show me what is under your shirt.

That's not it, said Emma. Then she changed her mind. That is it, she said.

What is wrong with me! the Dead Father shouted. You are making me feel like the Congress of Vienna!

Nonsense, said Emma, taking his hand. You are as good as you ever were. Or almost as good as you ever were.

Then come to bed with me, and I will whisper secrets in your ear. Powerful secrets.

Yes, Emma said, secrets, that's the second-best part, the secrets. The best part in my opinion is buying the furniture. Picking out the towels. The stainless steel. The rug. The potted plant. The bolster for the bedroom. The art object. The can opener.

Emma begins lachrymation (serious).

The can opener, she said, and the colander.

Why are you weeping? asked the Dead Father.

I was thinking about the salads, she said through her tears. Salad after salad. I am wonderful with salads.

Don't cry, please.

I am *so good* with salads, she said.

I am sure you are.

Only virgin imported fresh Italian olive oil. Sliced mushrooms and organic or uninstitutionalized tomatoes,

96

from a little place I know. And fronds, fronds of this and fronds of that. Coke, or snow some people call it, sprinkled on top along with salt, pepper, parsley, prepared mustard—

Come to bed, dear salad-head. Come to bed with me.

No I won't, said Emma. Pardon me for saying it but you are, you are, you are too old.

The Dead Father fell down on the ground and began chewing the dirt of the road.

Don't do that, dear friend, said Emma, plucking at his shoulder blades. It doesn't help.

16

Is everyone ready for the big dance?

How can we have a dance with only two women?

The women will just have to dance twice as hard.

Edmund claims the first dance.

No, that is for the Dead Father.

Happiness of the Dead Father.

The Dead Father and Julie dancing.

Edmund and Emma dancing.

Thomas performing upon the kazoo. Alexander upon the flute. Sam upon the banjo.

The "Immigration Waltz" performed.

Light from the bonfires.

Is that horseman still following us?

Yes, still.

You dance very well.

Yes I do dance very well. You dance pretty well.

Thank you. It's kind of hard to dance with this leg.

No really I mean it's very smooth, considering, but to tell the truth I really think this is a terrible dance.

Why?

There's nobody here.

I'm here.

Yes you but there's nobody else nobody new.

Do you want somebody new?

I always want somebody new.

What's so good about somebody new?

He's new. The newness.

That's a little insulting to those of us who are not new.

Tuff titty.

Why do you keep looking around?

Looking for somebody new.

Who sent out the invitations?

Who hired the band?

Who laid on the champagne?

Who hung the crepe paper?

Who lit the bonfires?

Wish they'd play something else.

What do you want to hear?

Something new.

Anything new?

Anything new.

How about "Midnight in Moscow"?

That's not new.

I know but it's pretty.

Can't dance to it it's too slow.

You're a little picky.

I am a little picky.

What?

I am a little picky. I know that. Tell me something new.

Don't know anything new.

I know that.

What?

Who are those people over there?

I don't know they may be the horseman who has been following us or some of his friends. Attracted by the music probably.

No they're not they're new. The horseman who has been following us is not new.

They seem sort of dark and furry.

Yes now that I look closely they're apes.

Yes I see what you mean they do appear to be apes.

One two three four five apes.

Yes they're tapping their feet to the music.

What's the tune.

It's the "Crabapple Stomp." I always liked that one.

Me too the only thing wrong with it is that it's not new, do you think they want to dance?

What?

Do you think they want to dance, the apes?

Ask them but maybe they would hold on too tightly.

I'll take a chance. They're new.

Maybe they would crush you with their incredibly powerful arms.

That would be new.

Probably they smell terribly.

That would be new too I'm tired of all you sweet-smellers.

What's that music?

That's the "Carborundum Waltz."

I was always fond of waltzes. I remember—

Look *she's* not scared of the apes she's asked one to dance.

He dances pretty well, for an ape.

Whose idea was having this dance in the first place?

It was the Dance Committee.

Well it breaks the monotony I suppose.

Yes I suppose it does that, in a sense.

I think some are male and some female the smaller ones are female, probably.

Yes they're slightly more graceful than the males.

I'm going to dance with one.

Leave me here in the middle of the floor?

It will be new.

Yes it will be new but I think it's slightly insulting to be dancing with a person and then leave that person alone in the middle of the floor and go off and dance with an ape.

100

You can have the dance after this one I'll write your name on my dance card.

I don't particularly want to dance with someone after that someone has been dancing with an ape.

Can you talk at all?
(Silence.)
Nothing?
(Silence.)
That's new.
(Silence.)
You apes live around here in the dense underbrush and move in and out among the trees seeking fruits and vegetables?
(Silence.)
Well you certainly are accomplished dancers except perhaps maybe you're holding me a little tight?
(Silence.)
Thank you that's better I suppose there's no point in asking you your name is it all right if I call you Hector?
(Silence.)
Are any of the females your wife or girl friend I mean, I suppose you dance with each other a lot at night or at festival times special occasions Hector there'll probably be repercussions about this the men don't like it I can see that would you like a plate of chicken or something oh I forgot you're not a meateater and probably it would be wrong of me to get you started but there are some little cakes and things and I think Kool-Aid or the equivalent things change their names so fast these days I'm not sure it's still called Kool-Aid may be just grape juice with a little something added to zip it up ouch! doesn't matter it was my fault where did you go to school excuse me that

101

was a dumb question it's just that when you're dancing you usually feel like you ought to make conversation and it's a little hard when the other person doesn't say anything.

(Silence.)

Well I've certainly enjoyed this dance it was new can I introduce you to one of the other members of our party who's a good dancer too lots of zest and a good personality you'll be surprised some people think she's prettier than I although that's not the sort of thing I can comment on can I ha ha just come on over here for a moment and I'll introduce you oh my she's dancing already well would you like to just sort of sit this one out what a grip, lightly, lightly, that's better you do understand quite a lot don't you an amazing amount considering would you excuse me for a moment I have to go to the ladies' room or I mean I must leave you for a moment Hector let go of my hand now I'll come back and we'll chat some more I promise Hector let go now don't be a—

This is Emma.

Emma, Hector.

Hector, Emma.

He likes to dance that I can tell you and don't be afraid he's really very sweet and quite new, a new experience I can promise you that.

Thomas approaches and asks Julie to dance.

Julie says that she is willing to dance with Thomas.

I saw you dancing with that ape.

Yes I was dancing with that ape his name is Hector I mean that's not really his name I don't suppose I just called him that.

Did you want to go to bed with him?

Never occurred to me I just wanted to try it, is all.

Are you sure you don't have a fantasy of going to bed with him you were dancing quite close I saw it.

Well he tends to hold on very tightly I don't think it's sexual so much I just think he likes to hold on to everything very tightly I mean I think that's the way he holds on to things. Very tightly.

Well it made me feel funny to see you dancing with him and talking to him and all that and you certainly looked like you were having a high old time.

Well he's very pleasant and sweet and believe me I had my work cut out for me just keeping the conversation going you've nothing to be jealous about nothing whatsoever I'm surprised at you jealous of an ape what's that music?

It's the "Registration Waltz." He certainly knows his way around a banjo.

Yes I didn't know he played banjo I knew he played guitar of course but I didn't know he played banjo.

I didn't even know we had a banjo but Sam has been carrying it all this way and a pocket cornet too you should see it it's only about eight or nine inches long but he gets a lot of sound out of it they're made in Warsaw he told me amazing how much musical talent you find around almost everybody can play something a little bit.

Yes I believe the Dead Father plays nine instruments he told me once what they were eight or nine but he can certainly make a banjo sing I think this was a good idea don't you everybody seems to be having a good time whose idea was it?

Edmund's. And Emma's.

What's that they're playing now?

It's the "Penetration Waltz" I believe.

And the apes coming, crashing I suppose but I don't care, gives you a feeling of newness always good to meet new people get an idea of what others are like new perspectives as it were I wish they could talk almost made a mistake and offered Hector some chicken salad probably a bad idea to get them started.

The Dead Father looks quite happy doesn't he almost benign one could almost forget about his wood chisels and all the rest of it seeing him sitting here keeping time with his mechanical leg and doing that what do they call it frailing I think I wonder where he learned that the old bastard knows a lot of different things you have to hand it to him product I suppose of his long years of—

Ouch! I'm sorry probably my fault do you want to get a little taste of something I'm thirsty look at that! that ape just knocked Edmund down now he's picking him up again now he's knocking him down again oh God we don't want a melee you'd better break it up maybe we could organize a lady-in-the-lake or something you try to get the apes in one line and I'll line up our people let me see twenty-three less the three playing plus five apes means roughly twelve on a side.

We'll need a caller, Thomas said, I'll do that, that means twelve on a side.

The lines formed. The trio begins "The Titanium Polka."

Honor your partner, Thomas said, all gather round, there's a great day comin', let's run it in the ground.

Emma and Hector do-si-do-ing down the lines.

This is the best dance I have ever been to! Emma exclaimed.

17

An outpost of civilization or human habitation. Dwellings in neat rows back to back to back to back. Children at play on roofs.

Where are the streets? asked the Dead Father.

There appear to be none, said Julie.

Perhaps tunnels in the earth?

Or maybe they squeeze between the houses, making themselves all teensy-weensy and not forgetting to gaze into the windows as they pass.

It is Planning, said Thomas, a New Town. One must achieve the rim to be killed by auto.

Circulation is not a big thing here, said a stander-by. Why is that man, that one of you, the distinguished-looking one, being dragged? What has he committed? Why are those nineteen puffing and sweating away, on the cable? Why are you three not puffing and sweating away on the cable? I do not understand your table of organization.

He is a father, said Thomas.

Terrible news, said the man, you can't bring him in here.

He is fatigued. *We* are fatigued. We can pay.

You'll have to deballock him and wipe your feet on the mat, said the man, whose face contained beardescules at odd points, such as the lips and center of the forehead.

Do you need a deballocking knife? Scissors? Razor? Paper cutter? Shard of glass? Letter opener? Fingernail clippers?

He is a sacred object, in a sense, Thomas said. No more of your bubblegum. Which way is the flophouse?

There are two, the citizen said. The good one and the bad one. The bad one has the best girls. The good one has the best pâté. The bad one has the best beds. The good one has the best cellar. The bad one has the best periodicals. The good one has the best security. The bad one has the best band. The good one has the best roaches. The bad one has the best martinis. The good one has the best credit cards. The bad one has the best table silver. The good one has the best views. The bad one has the best room service. The good one has the best reputation. The bad one has the best façade. The good one has the best chandelier. The bad one has the best carpet. The good one has the best bathrooms. The bad one has the best bar. The good one has the best Dun & Bradstreet. The bad one has the best portraits. The good one has the best bellmen. The bad one has the best potted plants. The good one has the best ashtrays. The bad one has the best snails. The good one has the best postcards. The bad one has the best breakfast. The good one—

Between the good one and the bad one, Julie said, there appears to be little choice.

There are also private houses but none large enough or foolish enough to attempt to accommodate your party, said the man. That thing there would scare the children out of their wigs, did they get but a glimpse of it.

He is talking about you, Emma said to the Dead Father.

The Dead Father beamed.

He says you'll frighten the children.

Happiness of the Dead Father.

Him, the citizen said, him can't be brought in without the fixing. I can lend you a Skilsaw.

I would prefer not to, said the Dead Father.

He prefers not to, Thomas told the citizen.

Well damn and blast, said the citizen, who would imagine otherwise? Yet a rule is a rule.

Edmund, Thomas called.

Edmund presented himself.

How would you like to buy a drink or so for this citizen of this fine community? Thomas asked. You may charge it to me.

Tremble of happiness running through Edmund from top to bottom (visible).

Edmund and the citizen off to the alehouse arm-in-arm.

Now, Thomas said, let's inspect the accommodations.

After looking at the good one, they chose the bad one.

Julie and Thomas in their room, sitting on the bed. Picture on the wall, *Death of Sigismur*.

Amazing how he holds on to his balls, said Julie, that is a curious thing, I don't understand it.

I understand it, said Thomas.

Doesn't know when it's time to hang it up, she said, how old do you think he is?

He claims one hundred and nine, said Thomas, but he may be stretching it. He may be shrinking it. I don't know.

Three of our people are clones I think.

Which three?

The three with the red hair and the limp.

Thomas lay back upon the bed.

What a disgusting idea, he said.

How is it that you gave him back his leg after you had whacked it off?

Purely practical. He staggers better with it. We have ends in view.

So we do, she said, so we do.

A knock on the chamber door.

Who's there? called a voice, from outside the door.

Shall we answer? Julie asked.

Who's there? the voice called again.

Who wants to know? Julie shouted.

107

There was a silence.

Peter, the voice said, at length.

Do we know anyone named Peter?

I know no one named Peter.

What do you want, Peter? she called.

I have to mist the plant, Peter called.

Thomas looked about him. A cactus sat on the dressing table.

Does one mist a cactus? Julie asked.

Let him in, Thomas said.

Julie opened the door.

Some people know what they are doing, Peter said, and some don't.

He began wrapping wet cheesecloth around the cactus.

Well there tall thin fellow, said Julie, why are you here?

I heard there were strangers. We don't often get strangers. I wanted to give it to you.

Wanted to give what to us?

He appears to be a dolt of some kind, Thomas said, sotto voce.

The book, Peter said.

What is the book about?

Peter had a frayed tattered disintegrating volume with showers of ratsnest falling out of it clutched to his chest.

It is a manual, he said. Might be of some small use to you. On the other hand, might not.

Are you the author? Julie asked.

Oh no, said Peter. I am the translator.

From what language was it translated?

It was translated from English, he said, into English.

You must have studied English.

Yes I did study English.

Is it long? Thomas asked, looking at the thin book.

It is not long, Peter said, and at the same time, too long.

Then, furiously:

Do you know what translators are paid?

Not my fault, Julie said, as with much else in the world, not my fault.

Pennies! Peter proclaimed.

Are you selling us this book?

No, Peter said nobly, I am giving it to you as a gift. It is not worth selling.

He unwrapped the cheesecloth from the cactus.

Edition of forty, he said, printed originally on pieces of pumpernickel. This is the second edition.

We must give you something, Thomas said, what can it be?

You are strangers, Peter said. Your approval would be enough.

You have it, said Julie. She kissed Peter on the forehead.

I am justified, Peter said, for the time being. I can struggle on, for the time being. I am reified, for the time being.

Exit of Peter.

He didn't ask much, said Thomas.

His bargaining position is not the best, Julie said. He is a translator.

They lay on their stomachs in the bed, looking at the book.

The book was titled *A Manual for Sons*.

The author was not credited.

"Translated from the English by Peter Scatterpatter" was found on the title page.

They began to read the book.

A
MANUAL
FOR SONS

TRANSLATED FROM THE ENGLISH BY
PETER SCATTERPATTER

(1)   Mad fathers
(2)   Fathers as teachers
(3)   On horseback, etc.
(4)   The leaping father
(5)   Best way to approach
(6)   Ys
(7)   Names of
(8)   Voices of
(9)   Sample voice, A
                    B
                    C
(10)   Fanged, etc.
(11)   Hiram or Saul
(12)   Color of fathers
(13)   Dandling
(14)   A tongue-lashing
(15)   The falling father
(16)   Lost fathers
(17)   Rescue of fathers
(18)   Sexual organs
(19)   Names of
(20)   Yamos
(21)   "Responsibility"
(22)   Death of
(23)   Patricide a poor idea,
         and summation

113

Mad fathers stalk up and down the boulevards, shouting. Avoid them, or embrace them, or tell them your deepest thoughts—it makes no difference, they have deaf ears. If their dress is covered with sewn-on tin cans and their spittle is like a string of red boiled crayfish running head-to-tail down the front of their tin cans, serious impairment of the left brain is present. If, on the other hand, they are simply barking (no tin cans, spittle held securely in the pouch of the cheek), they have been driven to distraction by the intricacies of living with others. Go up to them, and, stilling their wooden clappers by putting your left hand between the hinged parts, say you're sorry. If the barking ceases, this does not mean that they have heard you, it only means they are experiencing erotic thoughts of abominable luster. Permit them to enjoy these images for a space, and then strike them sharply in the nape with the blade of your tanned right hand. Say you're sorry again. It won't get through to them (because their brains are mush) but in pronouncing the words, your body will assume an attitude that conveys, in every country of the world, sorrow—this language they can understand. Gently feed them with bits of leftover meat you are carrying in your pockets. First hold the meat in front of their eyes, so that they can see what it is, and then point to their mouths, so that they know that the meat is for them. Mostly, they will open their mouths, at this point. If they do not, throw the meat in between barks. If the meat does not get all the way into the mouth but lands upon (say) the upper lip, hit them again in the neck, this often causes the mouth to pop open and the meat sticking to the upper lip to fall into the mouth. Nothing may work out in the way I have described; in this eventuality, you can do not much for a mad father except listen, for a while, to his babble. If he cries aloud, *"Stomp it, emptor!"* then you must attempt to figure out the code. If he cries aloud, *"The fiends have killed your horse!"* note down in your notebook the frequency with which the words "the" and "your" occur in his tirade. If he cries aloud, *"The cat's in its cassock and flitter-te-hee moreso stomp it!"* remember that he has already asked you once to "stomp it" and that this must refer to something you are doing. So stomp it.

Fathers are teachers of the true and not-true, and no father ever knowingly teaches what is not true. In a cloud of unknowing, then, the father proceeds with his instruction. Tough meat should be hammered well between two stones before it is placed on the fire, and should be combed with a haircomb and brushed with a hairbrush before it is placed on the fire. Iron lungs and cyclotrons are also useful for the purpose. On arriving at night, with thirsty cattle, at a well of doubtful character, one deepens the well first with a rifle barrel, then with a pigsticker,

116

then with a pencil, then with a ramrod, then with an ice pick, "bringing the well in" finally with needle and thread. Do not forget to clean your rifle barrel immediately. To find honey, tie a feather or straw to the leg of a bee, throw him into the air, and peer alertly after him as he flies slowly back to the hive. Nails, boiled for three hours, give off a rusty liquid that, when combined with oxtail soup, dries to a flame color, useful for warding off tuberculosis or attracting native women. Do not forget to hug the native women immediately. To prevent feet from blistering, soap the inside of the stocking with a lather of raw egg and steel wool, which together greatly soften the leather of the foot. Delicate instruments (such as surveying instruments) should be entrusted to a porter who is old and enfeebled; he will totter along most carefully. For a way of making an ass not to bray at night, lash a heavy child to his tail; it appears that when an ass wishes to bray he elevates his tail, and if the tail cannot be elevated, he has not the heart. Savages are easily satisfied with cheap beads in the following colors, dull white, dark blue, and vermilion red—expensive beads are often spurned by them. Non-savages should be given cheap books in the following colors, dead white, brown, and seaweed—books praising the sea are much sought after. Satanic operations should not be conducted without first consulting the Bibliothèque Nationale. When Satan at last appears to you, try not to act surprised. Then get down to hard bargaining. If he likes neither the beads nor the books, offer him a cold beer. Then—

Fathers teach much that is of value. Much that is not.

Fathers in some countries are like cotton bales; in others, like clay pots or jars; in others, like reading, in a newspaper, a long account of a film you have already seen and liked immensely but do not wish to see again, or read about. Some fathers have triangular eyes. Some fathers, if you ask them for the time of day, spit silver dollars. Some fathers live in old filthy cabins high in the mountains, and make murderous noises deep in their throats when their amazingly sharp ears detect, on the floor of the valley, an alien step. Some fathers piss either perfume or medicinal alcohol, distilled by powerful body processes from what they have been, all day long, drinking. Some fathers have only one arm. Others have an extra arm, in addition to the normal two, hidden inside their coats. On that arm's fingers are elaborately wrought golden rings that, when a secret spring is pressed, dispense charity. Some fathers have made themselves over into convincing replicas of beautiful sea animals, and some into convincing replicas of people they hated as children. Some fathers are goats, some are milk, some teach Spanish in cloisters, some are exceptions, some are capable of attacking world economic problems and killing them, but have not yet done so, they are waiting for one last vital piece of data. Some fathers strut but most do not, except inside; some fathers pose on horseback but most do not, except in the eighteenth century; some fathers fall off the horses they mount but most do not; some fathers, after falling off the horse, shoot the horse, but most do not; some fathers fear horses, but most fear, instead, women; some fathers masturbate because they fear women; some fathers sleep with hired women because they fear women who are free; some fathers never sleep at all, but are endlessly awake, staring at their futures, which are behind them.

The leaping father is not encountered often, but exists. Two leaping fathers together in a room can cause accidents. The best idea is to chain heavy-duty truck tires to them, one in front, one in back, so that their leaps become pathetic small hops. That is all their lives amount to anyhow, and it is good for them to be able to see, in the mirror, their whole life histories performed, in a sequence perhaps five minutes long, of upward movements which do not, really, get very far, or achieve very much. Without the tires, the leaping father has a nuisance value which may rapidly transform itself into a serious threat. Ambition is the core of this problem (it may even be ambition *for you*, in which case you are in even greater danger than had been supposed), and the çore may be removed by open-liver surgery (the liver being the home of the humours, as we know). I saw a leaping father in the park, he was two feet off the ground and holding a one-foot-in-diameter, brown leather object that he was pushing away from himself—a sin of some sort, I judged. He was aiming it at a net supported by a steel ring but the net had no bottom, there was no way on earth that the net would retain the sin, even if the father had been able to place the sin safely in the net. The futility of his project saddened me, but this was an appropriate emotion. There is something very sad about all leaping fathers, about leaping itself. I prefer to keep my feet on the ground, in situations where the ground has not been cut out from under me, by the tunneling father. The latter is usually piebald in color, and supremely notable for his nonflogitiousness.

119

The best way to approach a father is from behind. Thus if he chooses to hurl his javelin at you, he will probably miss. For in the act of twisting his body around, and drawing back his hurling arm, and sighting along the shaft, he will give you time to run, to make reservations for a flight to another country. To Rukmini, there are no fathers there. In that country virgin corn gods huddle together under a blanket of ruby chips and flexible cement, through the long wet Rukminian winter, and in some way not known to us produce offspring. The new citizens are greeted with dwarf palms and certificates of worth, are led (or drawn on runnerless sleds) out into the zocalo, the main square of the country, and their *augensheinlich* parentages recorded upon a great silver bowl, and their fingerprints peeled away, so that nothing can ever be proved. Look! In the walnut paneling of the dining hall, a javelin! The paneling is wounded in a hundred places.

I knew a father named Ys who had many many children and sold every one of them to the bone factories. The bone factories will not accept angry or sulking children, therefore Ys was, to his children, the kindest and most amiable father imaginable. He fed them huge amounts of

120

calcium candy and the milk of minks, told them interesting and funny stories, and led them each day in their bone-building exercises. "Tall sons," he said, "are best." Once a year the bone factories sent a little blue van to Ys's house.

The names of fathers. Fathers are named:
A'albiel
Aariel
Aaron
Aba
Ababaloy
Abaddon
Aban
Abathur
Abbott
Abdia
Abel
Abiou
Achsah
Adam
Adeo
Adityas
Adlai
Adnai
Adoil
Adossia
Aeon
Aeshma
Af

Afkiel
Agason
Agwend
Albert

Fathers have voices, and each voice has a *terribilità* of its own. The sound of a father's voice is various: like film burning, like marble being pulled screaming from the face of a quarry, like the clash of paper clips by night, lime seething in a lime pit, or batsong. The voice of a father can shatter your glasses. Some fathers have tetchy voices, others tetched-in-the-head voices. It is understood that fathers, when not robed in the father-role, may be farmers, heldentenors, tinsmiths, racing drivers, fist-fighters, or salesmen. Most are salesmen. Many fathers did not wish, especially, to be fathers, the thing came upon them, seized them, by accident, or by someone else's careful design, or by simple clumsiness on someone's part. Nevertheless this class of father—the inadvertent—is often among the most tactful, light-handed, and beauti-ful of fathers. If a father has fathered twelve or twenty-seven times, it is well to give him a curious look—this father does not loathe himself enough. This father fre-quently wears a blue wool watch cap, on stormy nights, to remind himself of a manly past—action in the North Atlantic. Many fathers are blameless in all ways, and these fathers are either sacred relics people are touched with to heal incurable illnesses, or texts to be studied, generation after generation, to determine how this idiosyncrasy may be maximized. Text-fathers are usually bound in blue.

The father's voice is an instrument of the most terrible pertinaciousness.

Sample voice A:
Son, I got bad news for you. You won't understand the whole purport of it, 'cause you're only six, a little soft in the head too, that fontanelle never did close properly, I wonder why. But I can't delay it no longer, son, I got to tell you the news. There ain't no malice in it, son, I hope you believe me. The thing is, you got to go to school, son, and get socialized. That's the news. You're turnin' pale, son, I don't blame you. It's a terrible thing, but there it is. We'd socialize you here at home, your mother and I, except that we can't stand to watch it, it's that dreadful. And your mother and I who love you and always have and always will are a touch sensitive, son. We don't want to hear your howls and screams. It's going to be miserable, son, but you won't hardly feel it. And I know you'll do well and won't do anything to make us sad, your mother and I who love you. I know you'll do well and won't run away or fall down in fits either. Son, your little face is pitiful. Son, we can't just let you roam the streets like some kind of crazy animal. Son, you got to get your natural impulses curbed. You've got to get your corners knocked off, son, you got to get realistic. They going to vamp on you at that school, kid. They going to tear up your ass. They going to learn you how to think, you'll get

your letters there, your letters and your figures, your verbs and all that. Your mother and I could socialize you here at home but it would be too painful for your mother and I who love you. You're going to meet the stick, son, the stick going to walk up to you and say howdy-do. You're going to learn about your country at that school, son, oh beautiful for spacious skies. They going to lay just a raft of stuff on you at that school and I caution you not to resist, it ain't appreciated. Just take it as it comes and you'll be fine, son, just fine. You got to do right, son, you got to be realistic. They'll be other kids in that school, kid, and ever' last one of 'em will be after your lunch money. But don't give 'em your lunch money, son, put it in your shoe. If they come up against you tell 'em the other kids already got it. That way you fool 'em, you see, son? What's the matter with you? And watch out for the custodian, son, he's mean. He don't like his job. He wanted to be president of a bank. He's not. It's made him mean. Watch out for that sap he carries on his hip. Watch out for the teacher, son, she's sour. Watch out for her tongue, it'll cut you. She's got a bad mouth on her, son, don't balk her if you can help it. I got nothin' against the schools, kid, they just doin' their job. Hey kid what's the matter with you kid? And if this school don't do the job we'll find one that can. We're right behind you, son, your mother and I who love you. You'll be gettin' your sports there, your ball sports and your blood sports and watch out for the coach, he's a disappointed man, some say a sadist but I don't know about that. You got to develop your body, son. If they shove you, shove back. Don't take nothin' off nobody. Don't show fear. Lay back and watch the guy next to you, do what he does. Except if he's a damn fool. If he's a damn fool you'll know he's a damn fool 'cause everybody'll be hittin' on him. Let me tell you 'bout that school, son. They do what they do 'cause I told them to do it. That's why they do it. They didn't think up those ideas their own selves. I told them to do it. Me and your mother who love you, we told them to do it. Behave yourself, kid! Do right! You'll be fine there, kid, just fine. What's the matter with you, kid? Don't be that way. I hear the ice-cream man outside, son. You want to go and see the ice-cream man? Go get you an ice cream, son, and make sure you get your sprinkles. Go give the ice-cream man your quarter, son. And hurry back.

B:
Hey son. Hey boy. Let's you and me go out and throw the ball around. Throw the ball around. You don't want to go out and throw the ball around? How come you don't want to go out and throw the ball around? I know why you don't want to go out and throw the ball around. It's 'cause you— Let's don't discuss it. It don't bear thinkin' about. Well let's see, you don't want to go out and throw the ball around, you can hep me work on the patio. You want to hep me work on the patio? Sure you do. Sure you do. We gonna have us a fine-lookin' patio there, boy, when we get it finished. Them folks across the street are just about gonna fall out when they see it. C'mon kid, I'll let you hold the level. And this time I want you to hold the fucking thing straight. I want you to hold it straight. It ain't difficult, any idiot can do it. A nigger can do it. We're gonna stick it to them mothers across the street, they think they're so fine. Flee from the wrath to come, boy, that's what I always say. Seen it on a sign one time, FLEE FROM THE WRATH TO COME. Crazy guy goin' down the street holdin' this sign, see, FLEE FROM THE WRATH TO COME, it tickled me. Went round for days sayin' it out loud

to myself, flee from the wrath to come, flee from the wrath to come. Couldn't get it outa my head. See they're talkin' 'bout God there, that's what that's all about, God, see boy, God. It's this God shit they try and hand you, see, they got a whole routine, see, let's don't talk about it, gets me all pissed off. It fries my ass. Your mother goes for all that shit, see, and of course your mother is a fine woman and a sensible woman but she's just a little bit ape on this church thing we don't discuss it. She has her way and I got mine, we don't discuss it. She's a little bit ape on this subject see, I don't blame her it was the way she was raised. Her mother was ape on this subject. That's how the churches make their money, see, they get the women. All these dumb-ass women. *Hold it straight kid.* That's better. Now run me a line down that form with the pencil. I gave you the pencil. What'd you do with the fuckin' pencil? Jesus Christ kid *find the pencil.* Okay go in the house and get me another pencil. Hurry up I can't stand here holdin' this all day. Wait a minute here's the pencil. Okay I got it. Now hold it straight and run me a line down that form. *Not that way dummy,* on the horizontal. You think we're buildin' a barn? That's right. Good. Now run the line. Good. Okay now go over there and fetch me the square. Square's the flat one, looks like a L. Like this, look. Good. Thank you. Okay now hold that mother up against the form where you made the line. That's so we get this side of it square, see? Okay now hold the board and lemme just put in the stakes. HOLD IT STILL DAMN IT. How you think I can put in the stakes with you wavin' the damn thing around like that? Hold it still. Check it with the square again. Okay, is it square? Now hold it still. Still. Okay. That's got it. How come you're tremblin'? Nothin' to it, all you got to do is hold one little bitty piece of one-by-six straight for two minutes and you go into a fit? Now stop that. Stop it. I said stop it. Now just take it easy. You like heppin' me with the patio, don'tcha. Just think 'bout when it's finished and we be sittin' out here

126

with our drinks drinkin' our drinks and them jackasses
'cross the street will be shittin'. From green envy. Flee
from the wrath to come, boy, flee from the wrath to come.
He he.

C:
Hey son come here a minute. I want you and me to have
a little talk. You're turnin' pale. How come you always
turn pale when we have a little talk? You *delicate*? Pore
delicate little flower? Naw you ain't, you're a *man,* son,
or will be someday the good Lord willin'. But you got to
do right. That's what I want to talk to you about. Now put
down that comic book and come on over here and sit by
me. Sit right there. Make yourself comfortable. Now, you
comfortable? Good. Son, I want to talk to you about your
personal habits. Your personal habits. We ain't never
talked about your personal habits and now it's time. I been
watchin' you, kid. Your personal habits are admirable.
Yes they are. They are flat admirable. I like the way you
pick up your room. You run a clean room, son, I got to
hand it to you. And I like the way you clean your teeth.
You brush right, in the right direction, and you brush *a
lot.* You're goin' to have good gums, kid, good healthy
gums. We ain't gonna have to lay out no money to get
your teeth fixed, your mother and I, and that's a blessing
and we thank you. And you keep yourself clean, kid,
clothes neat, hands clean, face clean, knees clean, that's
the way to hop, way to hop. There's just one little thing,
son, one little thing that puzzles me. I been studyin' 'bout
it and I flat don't understand it. How come you spend so

much time washin' your hands, kid? I been watchin' you. You spend an hour after breakfast washin' your hands. Then you go wash 'em again 'bout ten-thirty, ten-forty, 'nother fifteen minutes washin' your hands. Then just before lunch, maybe a half hour, washin' your hands. Then after lunch, sometimes an hour, sometimes less, it varies. I been noticin'. Then in the middle of the afternoon back in there washin' your hands. Then before supper and after supper and before you go to bed and sometimes you get up in the middle of the night and go on in there and wash your hands. Now I'd think you were in there playin' with your little prick, your little prick, 'cept you a shade young for playin' with your little prick and besides you leave the door open, most kids close the door when they go in there to play with their little pricks but you leave it open. So I see you in there and I see what you're doin', you're washin' your hands. And I been keepin' track of it and son, you spend 'bout three quarters of your wakin' hours *washin' your hands*. And I think there's somethin' a little bit *strange* about that, son. It ain't natural. So what I want to know is, how come you spend so much time washin' your hands, son? Can you tell me? Huh? Can you give me a rational explanation? Well, can you? Huh? You got anything to say on this subject? Well, what's the matter? You're just sittin' there. Well come on, son, what you got to say for yourself? What's the explanation? Now it won't do you no good to start cryin', son, that don't help anything. Okay kid stop crying. *I said stop it!* I'm goin' to whack you, kid, you don't stop cryin'. Now cut that out. This minute. Now cut it out. Goddamn baby. Come on now kid, get ahold of yourself. Now go wash your face and come on back in here. I want to talk to you some more. Wash your face, but don't do that other. Now go on in there and get back in here right quick. I want to talk to you 'bout bumpin' your head. You're still bumpin' your head, son, against the wall, 'fore you go to sleep. I don't like it. You're too old to do that. It disturbs me. I can hear you in there, when you go to bed, bump bump bump bump bump bump bump bump bump. It's disturbing. It's monotonous. It's a very disturbing sound. I don't like it. I don't like listenin' to it. I want you to stop it. I want you to get ahold of yourself. I don't like to hear that noise when I'm sittin' in here tryin' to read the paper or whatever I'm doin', I don't like to hear it and it bothers your mother. It gets her all upset and I don't like your mother to be all upset, just on accounta you. Bump bump bump bump bump bump bump bump bump, what are you, kid, some kind of animal? I cain't figure you out, kid. I just flat cain't understand it, bump bump bump bump bump bump bump. Dudden't hurtcha? Dudden't hurtcha head? Well, never mind about that right now. Go on in there and wash your face, and then come on back in here and we'll talk some more. And don't do none of that other, just wash your face. You got three minutes.

Fathers are like blocks of marble, giant cubes, highly polished, with veins and seams, placed squarely in your path. They block your path. They cannot be climbed over, neither can they be slithered past. They are the "past," and very likely the slither, if the slither is thought of as that accommodating maneuver you make to escape notice, or get by unscathed. If you attempt to go around one, you will find that another (winking at the first) has mysteriously appeared athwart the trail. Or maybe it is the same one, moving with the speed of paternity. Look closely at color and texture. Is this giant square block of marble similar in color and texture to a slice of rare roast

129

beef? Your very father's complexion! Do not try to draw too many conclusions from this; the obvious ones are sufficient and correct. Some fathers like to dress up in black robes and go out and give away the sacraments, adding to their black robes the chasuble, stole, and alb, in reverse order. Of these "fathers" I shall not speak, except to commend them for their lack of ambition and sacrifice, especially the sacrifice of the "franking privilege," or the privilege of naming the first male child after yourself: Franklin Edward A'albiel, Jr. Of all possible fathers, the fanged father is the least desirable. If you can get your lariat around one of his fangs, and quickly wrap the other end of it several times around your saddle horn, and if your horse is a trained roping horse and knows what to do, how to plant his front feet and then back up with small nervous steps, keeping the lariat taut, then you have a chance. Do not try to rope both fangs at the same time; concentrate on the right. Do the thing fang by fang, and then you will be safe, or more nearly so. I have seen some old, yellowed, six-inch fangs that were drawn in this way, and once, in a whaling museum in a seaport town, a twelve-inch fang, mistakenly labeled as the tusk of a walrus. But I recognized it at once, it was a father fang, which has its own peculiarly shaped, six-pointed root. I am pleased never to have met that father . . .

If your father's name is Hiram or Saul, flee into the woods. For these names are the names of kings, and your father Hiram, or your father Saul, will not be a king, but will retain, in hidden places in his body, the memory of kingship. And there is no one more blackhearted and surly than an ex-king, or a person who harbors, in the dark channels of his body, the memory of kingship. Fathers so named consider their homes to be Camelots, and their kith and kin courtiers, to be elevated or depressed in rank according to the lightest whinges of their own mental weather. And one can never know for sure if one is "up" or "down," at a particular moment; one is a feather, floating, one has no place to stand. Of the rage of the king-father I will speak later, but understand that fathers named Hiram, Saul, Charles, Francis, or George rage (when they rage) exactly in the manner of their golden and noble namesakes. Flee into the woods, at such times, or earlier, before the mighty scimitar or yataghan leaps from its scabbard. The proper attitude toward such fathers is that of the toad, lickspittle, smellfeast, carpet knight, pickthank, or tuft-hunter. When you cannot escape to the trees, genuflect, and stay down there, on one knee with bowed head and clasped hands, until dawn. By this time he will probably have drunk himself into a sleep, and you may creep away and seek your bed (if it has not been taken away from you) or, if you are hungry, approach the table and see what has been left there, unless the ever-efficient cook has covered everything with clear plastic and put it away. In that case, you may suck your thumb.

The color of fathers: The bay-colored father can be trusted, mostly, whether he is standard bay, blood bay, or mahogany bay. He is useful (1) in negotiations between warring tribes, (2) as a catcher of red-hot rivets when you are building a bridge, (3) in auditioning possible bishops for the Synod of Bishops, (4) in the co-pilot's seat, and (5) for carrying one corner of an eighteen-meter-square mirror through the city's streets. Dun-colored fathers tend to shy at obstacles, and therefore you do not want a father of this color, because life, in one sense, is nothing but obstacles, and his continual shying will reduce your nerves to grease. The liver chestnut-colored father has a reputation for decency and good sense; if God commands him to take out his knife and slice through your neck with it, he will probably say "No, thanks." The dusty-chestnut father will reach for his knife. The light-chestnut father will ask for another opinion. The standard-chestnut father will look the other way, to the east, where another ceremony, with more interesting dances, is being held. Sorrel-colored fathers are easily excitable and are employed most often where a crowd, or mob, is wanted, as for coronations, lynchings, and the like. The bright-sorrel father, who glows, is an exception: he is content with his glow, with his name (John), and with his life membership in the Knights of the Invisible Empire. In bungled assassinations, the assassin will frequently be a blond-sorrel father who forgot to take the lens cap off his telescopic sight. Buckskin-colored fathers know the Law and its mangled promise, and can help you in your darker projects, such as explaining why a buckskin-colored father sometimes has a black stripe down the spine from the mane to the root of the tail: it is because he has been whoring after Beauty, and thinks himself more beautiful with the black stripe, which sets off his tanned deer-hide color most wonderfully, than without it. Red roan-colored fathers, blue roan-colored fathers, rose gray-colored fathers, grulla-colored fathers are much noted for bawdiness, and this should be encouraged, for bawdiness is a sacrament which does not, usually, result in fatherhood; it is its own reward. Spots,

132

paints, pintos, piebalds and Appaloosas have a sweet dignity which proceeds from their inferiority, and excellent senses of smell. The color of a father is not an absolute guide to the character and conduct of that father but tends to be a self-fulfilling prophecy, because when he sees what color he is, he hastens out into the world to sell more goods and services, so that he may keep pace with his destiny.

Fathers and dandling: If a father fathers daughters, then our lives are eased. Daughters are for dandling, and are often dandled up until their seventeenth or eighteenth year. The hazard here, which must be faced, is that the father will want to sleep with his beautiful daughter, who is after all *his* in a way that even his wife is not, in a way that even his most delicious mistress is not. Some fathers just say "Publish and be damned!" and go ahead and sleep with their new and amazingly sexual daughters, and accept what pangs accumulate afterward; most do not. Most fathers are sufficiently disciplined in this regard, by mental straps, so that the question never arises. When fathers are giving their daughters their "health" instruction (that is to say, talking to them about the reproductive process) (but this is most often done by mothers, in my experience) it is true that a subtle rinse of desire may be tinting the situation slightly (when you are hugging and kissing the small woman sitting on your lap it is hard to know when to stop, it is hard to stop yourself from proceeding as if she were a bigger woman not related to you by blood). But in most cases, the taboo is observed, and additional strictures imposed, such as, "Mary, you are never to allow that filthy John Wilkes Booth to lay a hand upon your bare, white, new breast." Although in the modern age some fathers are moving rapidly in the opposite direction, toward the future, saying, "Here, Mary, here is your blue fifty-gallon drum of babykilling foam, with your initials stamped on it in a darker blue, see? there on the top." But the important thing about daughter-fathers is that, as fathers, they don't count. Not to their daughters, I don't mean—I have heard daughter-stories that would toast your hair—but to themselves. Fathers of daughters see themselves as *hors concours* in the great exhibition, and this is a great relief. They do not have to teach hurling the caber. They tend, therefore, to take a milder, gentler hand (meanwhile holding on, with an iron grip, to all the fierce prerogatives that fatherhood of any kind conveys—the guidance system of a slap is an example). To say more than this about fathers of daughters is beyond me, even though I am father of a daughter.

A tongue-lashing: "Whosoever hath within himself the deceivableness of unrighteousness and hath pleasure in unrighteousness and walketh disorderly and hath turned aside into vain jangling and hath become a manstealer and liar and perjured person and hath given over himself to wrath and doubting and hath been unthankful and hath been a lover of his own self and hath gendered strife with foolish and unlearned questions and hath crept into

134

houses leading away silly women with divers lusts and hath been the inventor of evil things and hath embraced contentiousness and obeyed slanderousness and hath filled his mouth with cursing and bitterness and hath made of his throat an open sepulcher and hath the poison of asps under his lips and hath boasted and hath hoped against hope and hath been weak in faith and hath polluted the land with his whoredoms and hath profaned holy things and hath despised mine holy things and hath committed lewdness and hath mocked and hath daubed himself with untempered mortars, and whosoever, if a woman, hath journeyed to the Assyrians there to have her breasts pressed by lovers clothed in blue, captains and rulers, desirable young men, horsemen riding upon horses, horsemen riding upon horses who lay upon her and discovered her nakedness and bruised the breasts of her virginity and poured their whoredoms upon her, and hath doted upon them captains and rulers clothed most gorgeously, horsemen riding upon horses, girdled with girdles upon their loins, and hath multiplied her whoredoms with her paramours whose flesh is as the flesh of asses and whose issue is like the issue of horses, great lords and rulers clothed in blue and riding on horses: this man and this woman, I say, shall be filled with drunkenness and sorrow like a pot whose scum is therein and whose scum hath not gone out of it and under which the pile for the fire is and on which the wood is heaped and the fire kindled and the pot spiced and the bones burned and then the pot set empty on the coals that the brass of it may be hot and may burn and that the filthiness of it may be molten in it, that the scum of it may be consumed, for ye have wearied yourselves with lies and your great scum went not forth out of you, your scum shall be in the fire and I will take away the desire of thine eyes. Remember ye not that when I was yet with you I told you these things?"

There are twenty-two kinds of fathers, of which only
nineteen are important. The drugged father is not important. The lionlike father (rare) is not important. The
Holy Father is not important, for our purposes. There is
a certain father who is falling through the air, heels
where his head should be, head where his heels should
be. The falling father has grave meaning for all of us.
The wind throws his hair in every direction. His cheeks
are flaps almost touching his ears. His garments are
shreds, telltales. This father has the power of curing the
bites of mad dogs, and the power of choreographing the
interest rates. What is he thinking about, on the way
down? He is thinking about emotional extravagance. The
Romantic Movement, with its exploitation of the sensa-
tional, the morbid, the occult, the erotic! The falling
father has noticed Romantic tendencies in several of his
sons. The sons have taken to wearing slices of raw bacon
in their caps, and speaking out against the interest rates.
After all he has done for them! Many bicycles! Many
gardes-bébés! Electric guitars uncountable! Falling, the
falling father devises his iron punishment, resolved not to
err again on the side of irresponsible mercy. He is also
thinking about his upward progress, which doesn't seem
to be doing so well at the moment. There is only one thing
to do: work harder! He decides that if he can ever halt
the "downturn" that he seems to be in, he will redouble
his efforts, really put his back into it, this time. The falling father is important because he embodies the "work
ethic," which is a dumb one. The "fear ethic" should be
substituted, as soon as possible. Peering skyward at his

endless hurtling, let us simply shrug, fold up the trampoline we were going to try and catch him in, and place it
once again on top of the rafters, in the garage.

To find a lost father: The first problem in finding a lost
father is to lose him, decisively. Often he will wander
away from home and lose himself. Often he will remain
at home but still be "lost" in every true sense, locked away
in an upper room, or in a workshop, or in the contemplation of beauty, or in the contemplation of a secret life.
He may, every evening, pick up his gold-headed cane,
wrap himself in his cloak, and depart, leaving behind, on
the coffee table, a sealed laundry bag in which there is
an address at which he may be reached, in case of war.
War, as is well known, is a place at which many fathers
are lost, sometimes temporarily, sometimes forever.
Fathers are frequently lost on expeditions of various kinds
(the journey to the interior). The five best places to seek
this kind of lost father are Nepal, Rupert's Land, Mount
Elbrus, Paris, and the agora. The five kinds of vegetation
in which fathers most often lose themselves are needle-
leaved forest, broad-leaved forest mainly evergreen,
broad-leaved forest mainly deciduous, mixed needle-
leaved and broad-leaved forest, and tundra. The five kinds
of things fathers were wearing when last seen are caftans,
bush jackets, parkas, Confederate gray, and ordinary
business suits. Armed with these clues then, you may
place an advertisement in the newspaper: *Lost, in Paris,
on or about February 24, a broad-leaf-loving father, 6'
2", wearing a blue caftan, may be armed and dangerous,*

137

we don't know, answers to the name Old Hickory. Reward. Having completed this futile exercise, you are then free to think about what is really important. Do you really want to find this father? What if, when you find him, he speaks to you in the same tone he used before he lost himself? Will he again place nails in your mother, in her elbows and back of the knee? Remember the javelin. Have you any reason to believe that it will not, once again, flash through the seven-o'clock-in-the-evening air? What we are attempting to determine is simple: Under what conditions do you wish to live? Yes, he "nervously twiddles the stem of his wineglass." Do you wish to watch him do so on into the last quarter of the present century? I don't think so. Let him take those mannerisms, and what they portend, to Borneo, they will be new to Borneo. Perhaps in Borneo he will also nervously twiddle the stem of, etc., but he will not be brave enough to manufacture there the explosion of which this is a sign. Throwing the roast through the mirror. Thrusting a belch big as an opened umbrella into the middle of something someone else is trying to say. Beating you, either with a wet, knotted rawhide, or with an ordinary belt. Ignore that empty chair at the head of the table. Give thanks.

On the rescue of fathers: Oh they hacked him pretty bad, they hacked at him with axes and they hacked at him with hacksaws but me and my men got there fast, wasn't as bad as it might have been, first we fired smoke grenades in different colors, yellow and blue and green, that put a fright into them but they wouldn't quit, they opened up on us with 81-mm. mortars and meanwhile continued to hack. I sent some of the boys out to the left to flank them but they'd put some people over there to prevent just that and my men got into a fire fight with their support patrol, no other way to do the thing but employ a frontal assault, which we did, at least it took the pressure off him, they couldn't continue to hack and deal with our assault at the same time. We cleaned their clocks for them, I will say that, they fell back to the left and linked up with their people over there, my flanking party broke off contact as I had instructed and let them flee unpursued. We came out of it pretty well, had a few wounded but that's all. We turned immediately to the task of bandaging him in the hacked places, bloody great wounds but our medics were very good, they were all over him, he never made a complaint or uttered a sound, not a whimper out of him, not a sign. This took place at the right arm, just above the elbow, we left some pickets there for a few days until the arm had begun to heal, I think it was a successful rescue, we returned to our homes to wait for the next time. I think it was a successful rescue. It was an adequate rescue.

Then they attacked him with sumo wrestlers, giant fat men in loincloths. We countered with loincloth snatchers —some of our best loincloth snatchers. We were successful. The hundred naked fat men fled. I had rescued him again. Then we sang "Genevieve, Oh, Genevieve." All the sergeants gathered before the veranda and sang it, and some enlisted men too—some enlisted men who had been with the outfit for a long time. They sang it, in the twilight, pile of damp loincloths blazing fitfully off to the left. When you have rescued a father from whatever terrible threat menaces him, then you feel, for a moment, that you are the father and he is not. For a moment. This is the only moment in your life you will feel this way.

The sexual organs of fathers: The penises of fathers are traditionally hidden from the inspection of those who are not "clubbable," as the expression runs. These penises are magical, but not most of the time. Most of the time they are "at rest." In the "at rest" position they are small, almost shriveled, and easily concealed in carpenter's aprons, chaps, bathing suits, or ordinary trousers. Actually they are not anything that you would want to show anyone, in this state, they are rather like mushrooms or, possibly, large snails. The magic, at these times, resides in other parts of the father (fingertips, right arm) and not in the penis. Occasionally a child, usually a bold six-year-old daughter, will request permission to see it. This request should be granted, once. But only in the early morning, when you are in bed, and only when an early-morning erection is not present. Yes, let her touch it (lightly, of course), but briefly. Do not permit her to linger or get too interested. Be matter-of-fact, kind, and undramatic. Pretend, for the moment, that it is as mundane as a big toe. And then calmly, without unseemly haste, cover it up again. Remember that she is being allowed to "touch it," not "hold it"; the distinction is important. About sons you must use your own judgment. It is injudicious (as well as unnecessary) to terrify them; you have many other ways of accomplishing that. Chancre is a good reason for not doing any of this. When the penises of fathers are semi-erect, titillated by some stray erotic observation, such as a glimpse of an attractive female hoof, bereft of its slipper, knowing smiles should be exchanged with the other fathers present (better: half smiles) and the matter let drop. Semi-erectness is a half measure, as Aristotle knew; that is why most of the penises in museums have been knocked off with a mallet. The original artificers could not bear the idea of Aristotle's disapproval, and mutilated their work rather than merit the scorn of the great Peripatetic. The notion that this mutilation was carried out by later (Christian) "cleanup squads" is untrue, pure legend. The matter is as I have presented it. The excited, mad, fully erect penis should be displayed only to the one who has excited it, for his or her lips, for the kiss of amelioration. Many other things can be done with the penises of fathers, but these have already been adequately described by other people. The penises of fathers are in every respect superior to the penises of nonfathers, not because of size or weight or any consideration of that sort but because of a metaphysical "responsibility." This is true even of poor, bad, or insane fathers. African artifacts reflect this special situation. Pre-Columbian artifacts, for the most part, do not.

The names of fathers: Fathers are named
  Badgal
  Balberith
  Baldwin
  Balthial
  Basus
  Bathor
  Bat Qol
  Bealphares
  Beli

Bigtha
Binah
Biqu
Birch
Bird
Blaef
Blake
Bludon
Boamiel
Bob
Bodiel
Bualu
Buhair
Bull
Butator
Byleth

I knew a father named Yamos who was landlord of the bear gardens at Southwark. Yamos was known to be a principled man and never, never, never ate any of his children no matter how dire the state of his purse. Yet the children, one by one, disappeared.

We have seen that the key idea, in fatherhood, is "responsibility." First, that heavy chunks of blue or gray sky do not fall down and crush our bodies, or that the solid earth does not turn into a yielding pit beneath us (although the tunneling father is sometimes responsible, in the wrong sense, for the latter). The responsibility of the father is chiefly that his child not die, that enough food is pushed into its face to sustain it, and that heavy blankets protect it from the chill, cutting air. The father almost always meets this responsibility with valor and steadfastness (except in the case of child abusers or thiefs of children or managers of child labor or sick, unholy sexual ghouls). The child lives, mostly, lives and grows into a healthy, normal adult. Good! The father has been successful in his burdensome, very often thankless, task, that of keeping the child breathing. Good work, Sam, your child has taken his place in the tribe, has a good job selling thermocouples, has married a nice girl whom you like, and has impregnated her to the point that she will doubtless have a new child, soon. And is not in jail. But have you noticed the slight curl at the end of Sam II's mouth, when he looks at you? It means that he didn't want you to name him Sam II, for one thing, and for two other things it means that he has a sawed-off in his left pant leg, and a baling hook in his right pant leg, and is ready to kill you with either one of them, given the opportunity. The father is taken aback. What he usually says, in such a confrontation, is "I changed your diapers for you, little snot." This is not the right thing to say. First, it is not true (mothers change nine diapers out of ten), and second, it instantly reminds Sam II of what he is mad about. He is mad about being small when you were big, but no, that's not it, he is mad about being helpless when you were powerful, but no, not that either, he is mad about being contingent when you were necessary, not quite it, he is insane because when he loved you, you didn't notice.

The death of fathers: When a father dies, his fatherhood is returned to the All-Father, who is the sum of all dead fathers taken together. (This is not a definition of the All-Father, only an aspect of his being.) The fatherhood is returned to the All-Father, first because that is where it belongs and second in order that it may be denied to you. Transfers of power of this kind are marked with appropriate ceremonies; top hats are burned. Fatherless now, you must deal with the memory of a father. Often that memory is more potent than the living presence of a father, is an inner voice commanding, haranguing, yes-ing and no-ing—a binary code, yes no yes no yes no yes no, governing your every, your slightest movement, mental or physical. At what point do you become yourself? Never, wholly, you are always partly him. That privileged position in your inner ear is his last "perk" and no father has ever passed it by.

Similarly, jealousy is a useless passion because it is directed mostly at one's peers, and that is the wrong direction. There is only one jealousy that is useful and important, the original jealousy.

Patricide: Patricide is a bad idea, first because it is contrary to law and custom and second because it proves, beyond a doubt, that the father's every fluted accusation against you was correct: you are a thoroughly bad individual, a patricide!—member of a class of persons universally ill-regarded. It is all right to feel this hot emotion, but not to act upon it. And it is not necessary. It is not necessary to slay your father, time will slay him, that is a virtual certainty. Your true task lies elsewhere.

Your true task, as a son, is to reproduce every one of the enormities touched upon in this manual, but in attenuated form. You must become your father, but a paler, weaker version of him. The enormities go with the job, but close study will allow you to perform the job less well than it has previously been done, thus moving toward a golden age of decency, quiet, and calmed fevers. Your contribution will not be a small one, but "small" is one of the concepts that you should shoot for. If your father was a captain in Battery D, then content yourself with a corporalship in the same battery. Do not attend the annual reunions. Do not drink beer or sing songs at the reunions. Begin by whispering, in front of a mirror, for thirty minutes a day. Then tie your hands behind your back for thirty minutes a day, or get someone else to do this for you. Then, choose one of your most deeply held beliefs, such as the belief that your honors and awards have something to do with you, and abjure it. Friends will help you abjure it, and can be telephoned if you begin to backslide. You see the pattern, put it into practice. *Fatherhood can be, if not conquered, at least "turned down" in this generation*—by the combined efforts of all of us together.

Seems a little harsh, Julie said, when they had finished reading.

145

Yes it does seem a little harsh, said Thomas.

Or perhaps it's not harsh enough?

It would depend on the experience of the individual making the judgment, as to whether it was judged to be too harsh or judged to be not harsh enough.

I hate relativists, she said, and threw the book into the fire.

18

The jolting of the road. The dust. The sweat. The ladies in conversation.

Break your thumbs for you.

That's your option.

Take a walk.

Snowflakes, by echoes, by tumbleweed.

Right in the mouth with a four-by-four.

His basket bulging.

I know that.

Hunger for perfection indomitable spirit reminds me of Lord Baden-Powell at times.

I know that.

Was there a message?

Buzzing in the right ball.

Sometimes forgets and uses too many teeth.

Pop one of these. Make you feel better.

What is the motivation?

I was suspicious of him from the first.

At the launching of his now rapidly fading career.

And in the poorest houses nuts are roasted and sweet brans.

Tattering leather and balding blue velvet.

Where can a body get a bang around here?

Certain provocations the government couldn't handle.

A long series of raptures and other spiritual experiences.

He was pleased.

Beside himself.

Something trembling in the balance.

Codpiece trimmed with the fur of silver monkeys.

He was pleased.

Feeling is what's important.

A gesture was made.

You were his second wife?

Second or third he lied rather often.

I wouldn't put it past him.

The child's interests were not protected.

Fill your face with bubblegum and suck your pacifier.

Saw a unicyclist in a brown hat.

I'm not into disgust.

Thought I heard a dog barking.

Handed him the yellow towel which he stuffed into his trousers.

Nobody ever died of it.

Worked them down over her hips.

Sometimes with music and sometimes with conversation.

Removing with a shout of triumph a whole live chicken.

He's not bad-looking.

I've noticed that.

We couldn't have been happier.

Mountain goats posing with their front legs together on the filing cabinets.

Feeling is what's important.

What was the room like?

Gray and the ceiling white.

What was the room like?

A shrug and a burst into tears.

Long gowns to the floor one yellow-white and one cooked-shrimp colored.

Something trembling in the balance.

Content to suck on a black tiptoe.

I applied for more time spreading the documents out before them.

I thanked the large black woman and withdrew.

Would have pissed elsewhere out of my sight if the conventions were then as they are now.

It's her own gut she's after.

He said I respected you when you were younger.

That's normal for cellists.

Got her a Rostropovich peg for her birthday.

She exhibited gratitude, blinked three times.

Mother.

Printed circuits reprinting themselves.

Did you let him see yours?

I assumed a brusque but friendly tone.

Probably afraid that she would drop it.

Probably afraid.

Got him right between the shoulder blades.

From such combinations in ancient days were sprung monsters.

This is not like me.

Wake up one dark night with a prick in your eye.

That's my business.

Approached it with a charming show of fastidious distaste.

That's my business.

Years not unmarked by hideous strains.

The letter a failure but I mailed it nevertheless.

That's your opinion.

Quite. That's my opinion.

Cracked halfhaired puckerfaced creature.

Mother.

Asked if I wanted to play. I noticed that all of the pieces were black.

I read about it in *Le Monde*.

He doesn't know what he's in for.

Sender of the sweet rain.

Keeps the corn popping.

The bourgeois press told stories.

The incredibly handsome waiter had been listening.

Carbon paper under the tablecloth all the while.

Knits the power grips.

Eats his kids they say.

Her red lips against the bone in my nose.

I can make it hot for you.

What is your totem?

The credit card.

When you are an old person you live in a small room small but neat and you don't have any cymbals any more they've taken your cymbals away from you.

It's a dirge not a dance.

Stop being petty, stop trying to cut each other's throat.

Always quick to call another woman beautiful.

Definite absolute negative influence.

And never does so if it is not true.

Hoping this will reach you at a favorable moment.

Some use camel saliva.

Teeth in dreams flaking away like mica.

They like to suck.

They do like to suck.

Sitting on some steps watching the tires of parked cars crack.

Shame, which has made marmosets of so many of us.

Mandrills watching from the sidelines with their clear, intelligent eyes.

Very busy making the arrangements.

Appeals to idealism.

Grocers wearing pistol belts.

It's perfectly obvious.

I was astonished to discover that his golden urine has a purple stripe in it.

It's no mystery.

A few severed heads on stakes along the trail.

Polished tubes carried by some of the men.

Not sure I understand what the issues are.
String quartets don't march very well.
Whip her britches into a white foam.
I didn't want to join, particularly, but felt it, in the last analysis, important.
Not wrong to be critical.
Half-a-scandal away.
Has a trickle-down effect on the brain.
Blushed like a blue dog.
Yes, after the war. I don't deny it.
You must have studied English.
That's one way of looking at it.
Wigwag me when you get a moment.
Never got the hang of it.
He's an excellent pianist.
We remind him at every opportunity.
Throwing our caps in the air.
The beatings were long ago and not irregular.
A truck or horses could have been used.
That's your opinion.
The son-of-a-bitch.
That's your opinion.
Elegant way of putting chairs here and there.
I don't think it's so damned elegant.
Walks along placidly thinking his own thoughts.
Remembering, leaving, returning, staying.
Look at the parts separately.
Get an exploded view as they call it.
Tea on the lawn then.
The lawn!
Villains from the right, heroes from the left.
When he was again in their company he could not help remembering what he had seen.
A boiled brain and a burnt one.
Millions of birds have accepted.
Darkening the skies above the walkers.
The main thing is to get moving.

Outside bright sunlight on the snow.
I can eat a good meal and look at a street.
You're safe with me.
Sometimes a picture or two in a museum.
Sometimes.
I don't mind hotel rooms.
Soldiers, horses, peasants, naked girls.
Playing a guitar.
He plays very well.
Hundreds of people squatting in a great half circle.
Throwing our caps in the air.
The son-of-a-bitch.
Control is the motif.
He made short work of them.
Is that a threat?
A vast barracks in very poor condition.
Carrying off caskets of municipal bonds.
Hers was a pretty fakey number.
Because the world's peoples are choking.
Dead infants fishermen found in their nets.
Blood Clot Boy, Water Jar Boy, all the heroes of the past.
Stumble at noon as in the twilight.
What they say in town is, he wore elevator shoes.
Wrote things on her in colored chalks.
Her eyes seemed to be scanning the company searching with a furtive yet sincere interest.
Sicker than Pascal himself in the opinion of some.
Drinking vodka from paper cups.
She had a flight of the imagination then.
Even I liked the faint memory.
Courting disaster.
What stories is she telling herself?
Said he had a board in his chest.
Dr. Margaux corrected what Dr. Elias could not.
Sometimes with music and sometimes with conversation.

The cello leaning against the wall.

Have some.

What is it?

Potato.

Thank you.

Handed him a yellow towel which he stuffed into his trousers.

I applied for more time spreading the documents out before them.

A thing he had done for the love of me.

Will you let him see it?

Hours in this position thinking I would suppose.

Except for rats and insects, woodworms and squirrels.

I noticed a tall young man who was speaking to your husband.

Got him right between the shoulder blades.

Psychologically punishing.

When I try to speak to her about it she turns the conversation, yawns or giggles.

Parts of hero all over.

He made short work of them.

Scratches her ass, good ankles.

Anything else of that nature?

Hanging by the hair.

There was a man walking on the tops of cars.

Some way to save the situation.

True love affairs of a lifelong character.

Anything else of that nature?

Wake up one dark night with a puckle in your eye.

We chat.

About what?

That's my business.

Then perhaps he regards you kindly.

Series of failed experiments.

You have performed well under difficult conditions.

Animals in which the brain strangles the esophagus.

Years not unmarked by hideous strains.

153

Willfully avoided gathering to myself the knowledge aforementioned.

And when not surly, pert.

The letter a failure but I mailed it nevertheless.

It's wonderful and reduces the prison population too.

I was surprised to see him in this particular bar.

Very young he's.

Parts of hero all over.

Many of them connected by legal or emotional ties.

Stares calmly at something a great distance away.

Clanging his balls for us.

Pop one of these if you'd like a little lift.

A ringbolt buried in the concrete, he tripped.

Embankments sewn with gracious blooms, heliotrope.

Not sure I understand what the issues are.

Do you want chocolate or strawberry?

Strawberry.

Strawberry's best.

That's your opinion.

Get a handle on it one way or the other.

Pressure has been continually building.

That's your opinion.

Your hands and tongue.

Where do you like it?

An elegant way of disposing warning sirens.

I don't think it's so damn elegant.

Bless me, Father, for I have sinned.

Riding the two-legged horses.

Gimping off into the future.

Warmly refused on all sides.

File after file of wooden soldiers marching through a low doorway. Got their heads knocked off.

You and I talked about this once.

There was brought forth and placed before him by four strong men a beef properly cooked over the flames.

There's just one thing a simple little rule.

Regarding their loved ones with hatred.

To partake of this al fresco party.
Where can a body get a pop around here?
Everyone was very enthusiastic.
He is a perpetual drudge restless in his thoughts.
He's not bad-looking.
The reindeer, man, and snowflakes were cut.
Tears some meat from his breast and puts it on a bun.
You're safe with me.
If this is what you believe you are wrong.
Dejected looks, flaggy beards, singing in the ears, old,
wrinkled, harsh, much troubled with wind.
Everyone is very enthusiastic.
Darkening the skies above the walkers.
Poring over diaries and memoirs for clues to the past.
Most people conceal what they feel with great skill.
Not getting anywhere not making any progress.
God may surprise me.
Outside there's bright sunlight on the snow.
Stumble at noon as in the twilight.
There'll always be another chance tomorrow.
Hoping that this will reach you at a favorable moment.
Old coins, statues, rolls, edicts, manuscripts.
Colder weather coming and then warmer.
Not getting anywhere not making any progress.
Control is the motif.
That and splashes.
Photo . . .

19

Nine o'clock?

Ten o'clock.

I have to have bed check for the men at ten o'clock. What about eleven o'clock?

I think I can make eleven o'clock. Let me look in my book.

She looked in her book.

Eleven o'clock, then, she said, writing a note in her book. Under the trees?

Under the stars, said Thomas.

The trees, said Julie, looks like rain.

If no rain, then the stars, said Thomas. If rain, then the trees.

Or the hedge, said Julie. Wet and dripping. Mulchy.

What are you arranging? asked the Dead Father. Could it be an assignation?

Nothing, said Julie. Nothing you should concern yourself about, dear old soul.

The Dead Father flang himself to the ground.

But I should have everything! Me! I! Myself! I am the Father! Mine! Always was and always will be! From whom all blessings flow! To whom all blessings flow! Forever and ever and ever and ever! Amen! Beatissime Pater!

He is chewing the earth again, Julie observed. One would think he would tire of it.

Thomas began singing, in a good voice.

The Dead Father stopped chewing the earth.

That is one I like, he said, wiping his mouth with the sleeve of his golden robe.

For *thine,* Thomas sang, in a good voice, is the kingdom, and the power, and the glo-ree, for-EVVVVVVV-VVVVVVV VVVVVVVV VVVVVVVV-er . . .

That is one I like, said the Dead Father, I have always liked that one.

Thomas stopped singing.

By the way, he said, let me have your passport.

Why? asked the Dead Father.

I'll take care of it for you.

I can take care of my own passport.

Many people lose or carelessly misplace their passports, Thomas said. I'll take care of it for you.

Very kind of you but not necessary.

A lost or misplaced passport is a very serious matter. Many people are extremely careless with their passports especially older people.

I've always been very careful with my passport.

Especially older people who are sometimes vague or forgetful, a concomitant of advancing age.

Are you suggesting I'm becoming senile?

Ghastly look of the Dead Father.

Oh no, said Thomas. Not senile. Not for a moment. I just thought it might be better if I took care of your passport. We are crossing frontiers and all that. Let me have your passport.

No, said the Dead Father. I will not.

I knew an old person once who lost or misplaced his passport, said Thomas. Stopped by the border police, at a certain border, he could not find or locate his passport. There he was at the border station, frantic, digging

157

through his suitcases, patting himself on the chest, turning out his pockets, and then back into the baggage. The amused tolerance of the border guards turning into impatience, others waiting behind him in line, assorted loafers and jeerers loafing and jeering. Not to mention members of his own party nervously drumming fingertips on every available surface. The entire group was forced to turn back and return to point of origin, all because this old coot had thought himself able to take care of his own passport.

The Dead Father reached inside his cloak and produced a worn green passport.

Thank you, said Thomas. You see? It's bent.

Inspection of passport in which sundry creases were seeable.

Only a little bent, said the Dead Father.

The individual's passport is the property strictly speaking of the governing government and therefore should not be bent, even a little. A bent passport makes suspect the competence of the passport holder.

I don't like this, said the Dead Father.

What? asked Julie. What, dear old man, don't you like?

You are killing me.

We? Not we. Not in any sense we. Processes are killing you, not we. Inexorable processes.

Inexorable inapplicable in my case, said the Dead Father. Hopefully.

"Hopefully" cannot be used in that way, grammatically, said Thomas.

You are safe, dear old man, you are safe, temporarily, in the mansuetude of our care, Julie said.

The what?

The mansuetude that is to say mild gentleness of our care.

I am surrounded by creepy murderous pedants! the Dead Father shouted. Unbearable!

Thomas handed the Dead Father the pornographic comic book.

Now now, he said, no outbursts. Read this. It will keep you occupied.

I don't want to be kept occupied, said the Dead Father. Children are kept occupied. I want to participate!

Not possible, said Thomas. Thank God for the pornographic comic book. Sit there and read it. Sit there with your back against that rock. Thank the Lord for what is given to you. Others have less. Here is a knapsack to place between your back and the rock. Here is a flashlight to read the pornographic comic book by. Edmund will bring your Ovaltine at ten. Count your blessings.

The trees. The stars. Each tree behaving well, each star behaving well. Perfume of nightscent.

Thomas lying on his back, cruciform.

Julie prowling the edges.

Julie kisses inside of Thomas's left leg.

Thomas remains in Position A.

Julie kisses Thomas on the mouth.

Thomas remains in Position A.

Julie back on her haunches with a hand between her legs.

Thomas watching Julie's hand.

Glistening in the hair between Julie's legs.

Slight movement of Julie's stomach.

Thomas watching Julie's hand (neck craned to see).

Julie kissing underside of Thomas's dipstick.

Cockalorum standing almost straight up but a bit of wavering.

Julie licks.

Pleasure of Thomas. Movement of Thomas's hips.

Julie lights cigarette.

Thomas remains in Position A.

Julie smokes looking at Thomas.

Julie smokes with one hand (second finger) moving up and down between her legs.

Various movements on Thomas's part. Trying to see.

Julie smokes. Offers cigarette to Thomas.

Thomas raises head, takes cigarette between lips. Two puffs.

Julie removes cigarette. Hand between legs.

Julie smokes looking at Thomas.

Thomas remains in Position A, as per the agreement. Julie's hand moving up and down between her legs. Thomas staring at Julie's hand.

Various movements on Thomas's part—lurches, mostly.

One of Julie's legs in the air.

Julie remaining just out of Thomas's reach. Thomas cruciform, as per the agreement.

Thomas's mowdiwort at 90 degree angle (roughly) to Thomas.

Julie sucks.

Thomas scratches nose with left hand, violating the agreement.

Julie's breasts dipping this way and that, as she sucks.

Thomas stares at breasts, straining and craning.

Julie stands and moves second finger between legs, gazing at Thomas.

Thomas makes sucking sounds.

Julie kneels astride Thomas's right leg, and rubs. Again and again and again.

Julie offers fingertips to Thomas, who licks.

Julie attends to Thomas's gadso, which is at a 90 degree angle (roughly) to Thomas.

Julie lies on one elbow twelve inches from Thomas and sips a whiskey. Hand between her legs.

Thomas staring at her hand, at her buttocks, stomach muscles.

In-and-out of Julie's stomach muscles. Hand between legs, eyes closed.

Thomas remains in Position A.

One of Julie's legs waving in the air.

160

Julie stands and then squats. Presenting greens to Thomas's cabbage tree.

Takes cabbage tree in hand. Use of cabbage tree as dildo.

Thomas staring at Julie's face.

Thomas remains in Position A, so as not to violate the agreement.

Julie attends to Thomas's bag-of-tricks for a long time.

Julie turns arsy-versy all cockalorum-kissing.

Thomas licks what there is to lick.

Happiness of Thomas. Happiness of Julie.

Movement of Julie's buttocks, to the right, to the left, and so on.

A short aria of three notes.

And so on and so on and so on and so on.

What time is it? asked Julie.

Almost one, said Thomas.

How much further?

Almost there, Thomas said. A day's journey, perhaps. Twenty-four hours at most.

Julie began to cry.

20

Thomas offered the Dead Father a document bound in blue paper.

What is it?

Read it, Thomas said.

It was a will.

It is a will, the Dead Father said, whose?

We thought it best that you take the precaution, Thomas said. Many people are inadequately prepared.

I don't want to make a will, said the Dead Father.

No one *wants* to make a will, said Thomas. Still it is a prudent step that we thought you ought to take, in your wisdom.

My wisdom, said the Dead Father. Infinite. Unmatched. Still, I don't want to make a will.

Prudence and wisdom being two of your strongest suits, Thomas said.

Dash my wig! said the Dead Father, I'll not do it. I'm too young.

Thomas looked up into the sky.

Of course it's entirely up to you, he said. If you wish to leave your affairs in rotten mishmashy cluttersome disarray . . .

I'm too young! the Dead Father said.

Of course you are, said Thomas, so are we all. Yet there is a vein in you that may pop at any time. I have identified it. Runs up the right leg and who knows, who knows where it wanders after it leaves the leg. Lurking potential embolisms menace it. I don't want to frighten you, but you get the picture.

By the Holy Goat, the Dead Father said, I will not.

Thomas waved his hands in the air suggesting exhausted patience and disinterested pursuit of what-is-right.

Who shall I leave it to? the Dead Father asked. Who is worthy?

I should say, no one. Perhaps the nation. The first step is the inventory. Can you give me some idea of what the estate consists of?

Vast, said the Dead Father. I have no idea. Consult my steward.

Your steward has been let go, said Thomas.

Luke? Luke gone? On whose authority?

It was thought best, Thomas said.

Then who is looking after things?

I believe his name is Wilfred, Thomas said.

But Wilfred is not Luke, the Dead Father said.

Best we could manage, said Thomas. You have no idea at all as to the size of your holdings?

Oh I have *some* idea, said the Dead Father. He produced a small black pocket notebook.

You're taking this down?

Thomas nodded.

The Dead Father cleared his throat.

Various lands in Saxony, he read aloud.

That's rather vague, Thomas said.

Um, said the Dead Father unperturbed, so it is. Let me continue. Certificates of deposit totaling—

Totaling what? asked Thomas.

They are all separate and distinct figures with no total listed, said the Dead Father. The sum would appear to be quite large, could one add it.

He turned a page.

163

A nut-brown maid, he read. Regina. The stereo. A pair of chatterpies. My ravens. A parcel of rental properties. Eleven rogue elephants. One albino. My cellar. Twelve thousand bottles more or less. Lithographs to be swallowed for sickness. Two hundred examples. My print collection, nine thousand items. My sword.

Your sword is gone, Thomas noted.

My sword is gone, said the Dead Father, but I have a spare sword, back in the city. My second-best sword. Jeweled hilt and all that.

A field of flowers outside Darmstadt. Wrinkleflowers. My greenhouses and potting sheds. Wilfred will know. Portrait busts of myself by Houdon, Minque, Planck, and Bowdoin. My napkin rings. Four thousand volumes of cabalistic literature. Cycladic figures to the number of one hundred eighteen. My gouges. The straight gouge, short bent gouge, long bent gouge, V gouge, U gouge, 5/32″ gouge, 3/8″ gouge. Four skew chisels. My box at the opera. My Bennie Moten records. My Thonet rocking chair. The regiment.

To whom will you leave the regiment?

Do you want it?

What would I do with the regiment? Thomas asked.

Parade it. Have regimental dinners. Fold and unfold the colors. Defend frontiers. Push into the Punjab.

Let us table the question, for the time being, said Thomas. Is there more?

Much, much, more, said the Dead Father, but let us lump it together under "incidentals." Do you want Regina?

Never having met the lady, Thomas said, I would say not. Also I am a witness and a witness cannot be a beneficiary. I do not wish to profit from this transaction in any way. I only wish to have everything tidy.

Tidy, said the Dead Father, what a way of putting it.

Julie will be a witness and Emma will be a witness and one of the men is, I have learned, a notary.

164

I shall place the regiment in trust for itself, said the Dead Father. That should take care of it. Have you the form?

Yes, Thomas said. Shall I read it?

Read it.

"This Trust is created upon the express understanding that the issuer, custodian, or transfer agent of any shares held hereunder shall be under no liability whatsoever to see to its proper administration . . ."

That's the way it begins?

No, it begins with a "Whereas." I'm reading you the part that doesn't sound right.

Read on.

". . . and that upon the transfer of the right, title, interest in and to such shares by any trustee hereunder, said issuer, custodian, or transfer agent shall conclusively treat the transferee as the sole owner of such shares. In the event that any shares, cash or other property—"

The regiment, for example, said the Dead Father.

". . . shall be distributable at any time under the terms of said shares, the said issuer, custodian, or transfer agent is fully authorized to pay, deliver, and distribute the same to whosoever shall then be the trustee hereunder, and shall be under no liability to see to the proper application thereof."

He paused.

Good deal of handwashing there, said the Dead Father. What paragraph is that?

Paragraph 4, said Thomas, perhaps you will like Paragraph 5 better. "I hereby reserve unto myself the power and right—"

Yes, said the Dead Father, I like that better.

"During my lifetime—"

No, said the Dead Father, I don't like it better.

Lifetimes and deathtimes, said Thomas, are what wills are about.

Yes, said the Dead Father, that's what I don't like, being reminded.

You need not bother with the details, Thomas said, you are fully protected, I assure you. The thing to do is sign it.

I'm too young. And who will beneficiate?

I care not a whit, said Thomas, pick someone. Or something.

Edmund, said the Dead Father.

Edmund?

He is the last, said the Dead Father, and the last shall be first.

Edmund?

I have made up my mind, said the Dead Father.

As you wish, said Thomas, we shall have to tell him about it very slowly, otherwise it will kill him.

Parcel the news out bit by bit, said the Dead Father. Begin with the napkin rings.

Thomas assembling the witnesses for the ceremony.

The notary said: Do you identify this document as your Last Will and Testament, do you wish it to be so regarded, and have you signed it of your own free will?

Yes, said the Dead Father. Sort of.

What was that? asked the notary.

More or less yes, said the Dead Father.

Well was it yes or was it not yes?

It was yes, I guess.

The notary looked at Thomas.

I heard "yes," said Thomas.

The notary said: And have you requested that these persons witness your signature and make an affidavit concerning your execution of this Will?

I have, said the Dead Father.

The witnesses will please raise their right hands. Do each of you individually declare under oath that the Dead Father has identified this document as his Last Will and Testament and stated that he wished it to be so regarded?

He has, said Thomas, Julie, and Emma.

166

Has he signed it in your presence and did he at that time appear to be of sound mind and legal age and free of undue influence?

Was he ever of sound mind? Julie wondered aloud. As you and I would define it? Strictly speaking?

A mind of his own, Thomas said, that much is clear.

I always liked him, said Emma.

Will the witnesses respond to the question?

Yes, said the witnesses, he has and did.

Have you in his presence and in the presence of each other, affixed your signatures?

We have.

The thing is done, said the notary, where is the brandy?

Thomas poured brandy for all hands.

This should make you feel good, the notary said to the Dead Father. A prudent step. Prudent, prudent.

Rage of the Dead Father.

Prudent is shit!

21

You two children have walked me many kilometers, said the Dead Father.

So we have, said Julie.

With scant regard for your own comfort. Your own projects. Of which you doubtless have a great many. You have labored on and on and on and on. For me.

That is the case, said Julie.

What of yourselves? Your two lives?

In what sense, what?

What purpose? What entelechy? What will you do with yourselves when it is all over?

Julie looked at Thomas.

What will we do with ourselves when it is all over?

Thomas shook his head.

I'd rather not answer that question if you don't mind, she said.

Why not?

I haven't an answer.

I know that, the Dead Father said.

One would think one would be able to answer a question of that kind wouldn't one.

One would.

Disagreeable not to have a ready and persuasive answer intelligible to all.

I can imagine.

Could be answered possibly in terms of the kind of life one has imagined for oneself. Or in terms of what one is actually doing.

Both good choices, said the Dead Father. Also their congruence or non-congruence would be of interest.

Ugh! said Julie.

I hope I haven't spooked you.

I'd say you rather have.

Older people don't really like younger people, the Dead Father said.

A person on horseback approaching the group.

It is that one who has been following us, said Julie.

I wonder who it is, said Emma.

I know who it is, Thomas said. It is Mother.

The horse halted. Mother sitting on the horse.

Mother, Thomas said, we need some things from the store.

Yes, Mother said.

A ten-pound bag of flour. The unbleached.

Mother produced a pencil and an envelope.

Ten-pound bag of the unbleached, she said.

We need garlic, bacon, tonic water, horseradish, cloves, chives, and chicory.

Garlic, bacon, tonic water, horseradish, cloves, chives, chicory.

We need cigarettes, chili powder, silver polish, mayonnaise, Lysol, croutons, and chutney.

Cigarettes, chili powder, silver polish, mayonnaise, Lysol, croutons, chutney.

We need eggs, butter, peanut oil, vermouth, beef bouillon, and barbecue sauce.

Eggs, butter, peanut oil, vermouth, beef bouillon, barbecue sauce.

We need scouring powder, hand soap, lighter fluid, Fig Newtons, and tennis balls.

Scouring powder, hand soap, lighter fluid, Fig Newtons, tennis balls. Is that it?

That's it.

Very well, Mother said.

Thank you, Mother.

Mother reined her horse about and rode away.

I don't remember her very well, said the Dead Father. What was her name?

Her name was Mother, Thomas said, let me have your keys, please.

My keys?

Yes let me have your keys.

I need my keys.

Let me have them, please.

Without my keys I can't open anything.

I will keep them safe for you.

There are things I need my keys for, the Dead Father said. Things I need to open and close. Lock and unlock. Shut and unshut. Start and stop.

I will keep them safe for you.

I feel very uncomfortable without my keys! the Dead Father said.

They call it stormy Monday but Tuesday's just as bad, Thomas said, your keys.

The Dead Father gave Thomas his keys.

22

AndI. EndI. Great endifarce teeterteeterteetertottering. Willit urt. I reiterate. Don't be cenacle. Conscientia mille testes. And having made them, where now? what now? Mens agitat molem and I wanted to doitwell, doitwell. Elegantemente. Ohe! jam satis, AndI. Pathetiqularly the bumgrab night and date through all the heures for the good of all. The Father's Day to end all. AndI understand but list, list, let's go back. To the wetbedding. To the dampdream. AndI a oneohsevenyearold boy, just like the rest of them. Pitterpatter. I reiterate&reiterate&reiterate&reiterate, pitterpatter. Remember some old Papsday when heaped all round with gifties, the delegations presenting themselves, the musicking, quantuscumque, I'm a jollygood jollygood, pip of a pap, loved and rererespected by all. Endjoying the endthusiasm which your endtente has endgendered. All kettlecooking they were that Papsday and bonfiring and bellringing and carnalvailing, AndI the papinjay of the day, laurelheaded and goldenrobed and homaged to the skies. They came to AndI in their dozensandhundreds and did their kneebends, AndI most rightly and graciously and sweetly reiteratingandreiteratingandreiterating. The leader of the delegations mumbling something about maidens, how many maidens? AndI replied that Old AndI not so interested in maidens as formerly. Quantum mutatus illo!

he said but seriouslynowseriouslynow how many maidens and how bedecked? AndI repeated that I was not so maidenminded as formerly but as a gesture in the direction of custom and tradition and honoring the old ways I would accept would reluctantly accept ex abundantia one with red hair and one with hair black as carbon and one with brown soft hair and one blond as corntassel nil consuetudine majus and one with two breasts and one who excelled in the art of falconry and one who was a philosopher and one who was by nature sad in the cast of her mind et cetera et cetera et cetera total of forty-four for Papsmearing that Papsday. They came to my couch that eve all lovely and giddygay and roaratorious and tumtickling AndI paprikaed many papooses that night. I the All-Father but I never figured out figured out wot sort of animal AndI was. Endshrouded in endigmas. Never knew wot's wot. I reguarded my decisions and dispositions but there wasn't timeto timeto timeto. Endmeshed in endtanglements. There were things I never knew what made the pavement gray and what made the giant monuments move back and forth on the far horizon ceaselessly night and day on the far horizon and what made the leaves fibrillate on the trees and what comity meant and what made the heart stop and how unicorns got trapped in tapestries, these things I never learned. But AndI dealt out 1,856,700 slaps with the open hand and 22,009,800 boxes on the ear. Son, I'm not gonna hitya. I'm not gonna hitya unless you force me to it. Little cocksucker. Ceaselessly night and day for the good of all. AndI never wanted it it was thrust upon me. Feckless endangerment. Not a healthy endvironment. Reiterateandreiteratethattothebestofmyknowledgeandbelief I was Papping as best I could like my AndI before me palmam qui meruit ferat. It could have been otherwise. I could have refused it. Could have abjured it. Coastered along goodguying way through the world. Running a little shop somewhere, some little malmsey&popsicle place. Endeavoring to meet ends. To the bicker end. Endocardial endocarditis. Enow-enowenow don't want to undertake the OldPap yet. Let's have a party. Pap in on a few old friends. Pass the papcorn. Wield my pappenheimer once again. Old Angurvadal! Companion of my finest hours! Don't understand! Don't want it! Fallo fallere fefelli falsum! My broad domainasteries! Pitterpatter. Thegreatestgoodofthegreatestnumber was a Princeapple of mine. I was compassionate, insofarasitwaspossibletobeso. Best I cud I did! Absolutely! No dubitatio about it! Don't like! Don't want! Pitterpatter oh please pitterpatter

23

They came then to a large gap in the earth surrounded by hundreds and hundreds of people holding black umbrellas. Rain. The men laying down the cable.

This is it, said Thomas.

What is it? asked the Dead Father.

This.

This large excavation? asked the Dead Father.

Yes.

Julie looking away.

They straggled up the edge of the excavation.

Who has dug this great hole in the ground? asked the Dead Father. What is to be builded here?

Nothing, Thomas said.

How long it is, the Dead Father observed.

Long enough, said Thomas, I think.

The Dead Father looked again at the hole.

Oh, he said, I see.

And these, he asked, indicating the mourners, are they hired or volunteers?

Wished to pay their respects, said Thomas.

Great wreaths of every kind of flower standing about on stands.

No Fleece? asked the Dead Father.

Thomas looked at Julie.

She has it?

Julie lifted her skirt.

Quite golden, said the Dead Father. Quite ample. That's it?

All there is, Julie said. Unfortunately. But this much. This where life lives. A pretty problem. As mine as yours. I'm sorry.

Quite golden, said the Dead Father. Quite ample.

He moved to touch it.

No, said Thomas.

No, said Julie.

I'm not even to touch it?

No.

After all this long and arduous and if I may say so rather ill-managed journey? Not to touch it? What am I to do?

You are to get into the hole, said Thomas.

Get into the hole?

Lie down in the hole.

And then you'll cover me up?

The bulldozers are just over the hill, Thomas said, waiting.

You'll bury me alive?

You're not alive, Thomas said, remember?

It's a hard thing to remember, said the Dead Father. I don't want to lie down in the hole.

Few do.

Rain falling on all of the bystanders. Emma with kerchief to eyes. Julie standing with hands hiking up skirt.

Just once to place my hand on it? asked the Dead Father. Last request?

Denied, said Thomas. Unseemly.

Julie moved to the Dead Father, restoring her clothes.

My dear, she said, my dearest, lie down in the hole. I'll come and hold your hand.

Will it hurt?

Yes it will, she said, but I'll come and hold your hand.

That's all? said the Dead Father. That's the end?

Yes, she said, but I'll come and hold your hand.

That's the best you can do?

Yes, she said, I never do less than the best I can do, I'll come and hold your hand.

No more after this?

Don't believe so, said Thomas, can I help you off with the loop?

Together they maneuvered the loop from the Dead Father's torso.

I wasn't really fooled, said the Dead Father. Not for a moment. I knew all along.

We knew you knew, said Thomas.

Of course I had hopes, said the Dead Father. Pale hopes.

We knew that too.

Did I do it well? asked the Dead Father.

Marvelously well, said Julie. Superbly. I will never see it done better.

Thank you, said the Dead Father. Thank you very much.

Thomas placed his hand on the Fleece, outside the skirt.

It is lovely, said the Dead Father. I am covered with admiration.

And soon, with good black earth, said Julie. Sad necessary—

Oh to be alive, the Dead Father said, for one moment more.

That we can arrange, said Thomas. Two, if you wish.

The Dead Father stretched his great length in the hole. Skittering of black earth upon the great carcass, from the edges.

I'm in it now, said the Dead Father, resonantly.

What a voice, said Julie, I wonder how he does it.

She knelt and clasped a hand.

Intolerable, Thomas said. Grand. I wonder how he does it.

I'm in the hole now, said the Dead Father.
Julie holding a hand.
One moment more! said the Dead Father.
Bulldozers.

For a complete list of books available from Penguin in the United States, write to Dept. DG, Penguin Books, 299 Murray Hill Parkway, East Rutherford, New Jersey 07073.

For a complete list of books available from Penguin in Canada, write to Penguin Books Canada Limited, 2801 John Street, Markham, Ontario L3R 1B4.